LOST DREAMS

LAST STAND

EPISODE ONE

BLAZE WARD

KNOTTED ROAD PRESS

Packmule

Persephone

Additional Alexandria Station Stories

The Story Road

Siren

Two Bottles of Wine With A War God

The Science Officer Series Season One

The Science Officer

The Mind Field

The Gilded Cage

The Pleasure Dome

The Doomsday Vault

The Last Flagship

The Hammerfield Gambit

The Hammerfield Payoff

The Bryce Connection

The Science Officer Series Season Two

Alien Seas

Buried Among the Stars

Captain Navarre

Captain Daring

Revoked

Returned

Reborn

The Lazarus Alliance

Escape

Return

Rebellion

Revolution

Liberation

Retribution

Alliance

Shadow of the Dominion

Longshot Hypothesis

Hard Bargain

Outermost

Dominion-427

Phoenix

Princess Rualoh

The Handsome Rob Gigs

Can't Shoot Straight Gang

Can't Shoot Straight Gang Returns

Hunting Handsome Rob

Handsome Rob, Assassin

Earth Force Sky Patrol

Birth of the Star Dragon

Flight of the Star Dragon

Call of the Star Dragon

Shadow of the Star Dragon

Trial of the Star Dragon

Hunter Bureau

Mirrors

Latency

Pleasure Model

Inhuman

Fairchild

Fairchild

Strawberry Dragon

Contents

Scene One — 1
Scene Two — 7
Scene Three — 11
Scene Four — 21
Scene Five — 25
Scene Six — 29
Scene Seven — 33
Scene Eight — 45
Scene Nine — 49
Scene Ten — 59
Scene Eleven — 65
Scene Twelve — 73
Scene Thirteen — 79
Scene Fourteen — 87
Scene Fifteen — 91
Scene Sixteen — 103
Scene Seventeen — 111
Scene Eighteen — 119
Scene Nineteen — 133

Read More — 141
About the Author — 143
About Knotted Road Press — 145

Scene One

TESSA GLANCED OVER WHEN WYATT STARTED MUTTERING under his breath. The bridge of her little star freighter *Last Stand* was crowded with three of them in here, so Tessa was close enough to listen to Wyatt bitching. Or punch him in the mouth.

It *was* Wyatt.

Fin flew and didn't look up. But he also knew Wyatt. They'd been together as a team for more than two years now. Or rather, Tessa had been married to Fin and co-owner of the Randovall Nucleonautics Light Tumbrel named *Last Stand* for three years. Wyatt Nakada had come along a bit later.

Bit of a complication when she and Fin had been getting chased across the Hawkswold Sector by some bounty hunters over something of a misunderstanding and Wyatt had gotten himself crossways with a different set of armed hooligans and they'd all ended up at the same saloon one afternoon.

A quick consensus of purpose, a little gunplay, and they'd all gotten away.

She listened to the man grumble. He was always like this.

"Say it," Tessa ordered, looking over.

She was the captain of the vessel and the crew. Fin liked to tell anyone and everyone that he was a happily kept man. Wyatt pretended to be dumber than he was so nobody asked him to take on responsibilities for anything bigger than laundry or dishes. The man couldn't cook worth a damn.

Wyatt stopped watching the horizon out the front windshield and turned hard eyes towards her.

"Have we considered going straight?" he asked in a sour, grumbly voice.

Tessa wanted to laugh at those words coming from him, but she held her peace.

Fin did laugh, but those two had a weird relationship.

"We tried that, Big Guy," her husband reminded both of them on the small bridge as he dove the ship out of the sky. "Didn't work all that well as I recall. Too many people out there. Not enough work after the war. Assholes in charge like folks desperate enough to ignore laws."

Wyatt looked like he'd sucked a lime dry.

"Spill," Tessa said, softening her tone.

Wyatt could be a son of a bitch. An amoral, mercenary punk of a man, but he also sent a significant portion of his paycheck home to his mother on a monthly basis. Claimed she needed it to survive, with his dad dead. He'd been a loyal crew member for two years at this point, prickliness and grumbling notwithstanding.

And he was big and strong, a giant who loomed over most people.

"Got a bad feeling, boss," he finally said. "Dunno why. Just do."

"Somebody wake up on the wrong side of the palace

this morning?" Fin asked brightly. Teasing the big man. Not many people could get away with that. Fin was one of them.

Wyatt was one of the biggest humans Tessa had ever met. Shade under two meters. Hundred and twenty kilos before gear. Black hair short on his head and thick like a pelt everywhere else she'd seen. Couple of days of stubble on his face. Much lighter skin than Tessa, almost pale, but he was from Lorastir, and she had come from one of the darker minority groups of Zaddinul, back in the before.

Fin, on the other hand, was pretty and blond. Kept his Van Dyke trimmed and precise. Twenty-five centimeters shorter than Wyatt and only barely more than half as heavy. Ten centimeters shorter than Tessa.

Fin was better dressed, too, but Wyatt preferred to look like a grizzled merc in the field, while Fin was snappy today with his Plus Four breeks in a moss green, accessorized by a bright blue dress shirt with the sleeves rolled up.

Tessa had turned up the heat on the bridge before they'd dropped out of orbit. *Orvan* was hotter than comfortable over most of the surface, and the place they were headed was in the deep desert. Fin usually kept his flight deck chilly enough to wear his favorite fur-lined jacket when he flew, and she didn't need the temperature extremes on top of everything else today.

Wyatt rolled his eyes and scowled at Fin, but there was nothing behind it. Tessa had broken both of them to the bit early on, so the teasing was genial these days. It was only outsiders who got the sharp edge of anyone's tongue.

"It's a job," she reminded Wyatt. "Pitiful few of those floating around these days, so we need to keep the folks with money happy."

Wyatt shrugged.

"Yes," she continued. "I know we have Abigail renting part of the flight deck and paying us a nice monthly fee to fly her around this whole sector, but that just barely keeps us in food and parts. So we gotta do things like this. Don't tell me you're developing a conscience, Wyatt Nakada."

That got the start of an angry rise out of him. A flash of hardness that faded just as quickly before he chuckled.

As intended.

"Shit, no," he countered. "Just a bad feeling. It'll pass."

"Well, if you're feeling better, there's a jar of pickles in the cupboard behind you," Fin spoke up. "Wanna open it for me? You know how I love fresh pickles when I fly."

Another roll of the eyes as Tessa watched, but the big fellow opened a compartment and pulled out a jar. Part of the batch from last fall. Sealed damned tight, too, since they had to be able to withstand canning, resting, and the occasional stretch of zero gravity when something on the ship broke.

Wyatt gripped it and twisted with an audible pop, then screwed it down a little and handed it over Fin's shoulder.

"Thank you," Fin grinned with his voice, taking the jar and sliding it into the coffee mug holder.

One hand came off the big piloting wheel and two delicate fingers dipped in like a hummingbird feeding to emerge with a quarter slice of what Fin considered vinegary dill heaven. Tessa wasn't as deeply entranced with pickles, but you did what you had to in order to preserve the fresh produce that came out of the pots and hydroponics aft. Or trade with other ships that had surpluses so you got prizes.

Fin munched and hummed as he flew.

"Okay, gang," he said around a mouthful. "We're coming in. Still over the horizon from our target, but I'm not even picking up ground-based weather radar right now, so we appear to be alone. Ought to be on the ground in about ten minutes."

Tessa nodded to Wyatt, then leaned over to kiss her husband on the top of his head.

Wyatt grumbled some more, then headed down the stairs to the main deck. Tessa was down a few steps later and caught up with him as they reached the cargo bay aft and opened up the secret compartment that held the armory.

Doomripper was there, Wyatt's big, ugly, 6mm military surplus Corwin Arms G-77 assault rifle. Matte black and tougher looking than the man holding it, if that was possible. Wyatt slung it across his back, then pulled out his pistol, *Brunhilde*, a Bokov B-41 13mm semi-automatic that only somebody big would carry.

He looked like a merc with all that, plus the armored jacket he was going to wear in spite of temperatures approaching forty degrees Celsius out there.

Tessa waited for him to step aside before she grabbed her Kuznetsov 11mm Tactical (double action) Revolver, wrapping the belt around her waist and tying the holster around her thigh.

Corwin Arms Model 27 11mm lever action carbine with 50-cm barrel was next. She cycled the lever just enough to confirm that there was a bullet in the chamber, then closed it and dropped the hammer carefully.

"Why don't you upgrade from that ancient piece of junk?" Wyatt asked, nodding to the carbine in her hands like a cradled child.

"Because it will take any crap ammunition I can find," she reminded him. "Same stuff goes in the pistol as well. How many calibers do you have to carry around?"

He grumbled "three" under his breath. 6mm for the rifle, plus the 24mm grenades he could fire out of the top barrel when he found them. Then the 13mm stuff for his auto-pistol.

Tessa preferred a single line of bullets across the back of her waist and a speed loader in a pouch opposite the iron. Made you stop and consider your target, instead of hosing down a situation and hoping you hit something.

Wyatt usually did hit, but keeping that boy in ammunition had been so expensive she'd made him start paying for it himself. Without nearly a big enough raise to offset the difference.

He was learning, slowly.

She kept the 11mm.

"Fellow travelers, if you will bring your tray tables to the upright position, we are on final approach," Fin announced over the intercom like a commercial pilot. "We at Barton/Sladek Spaceways would like to thank you for flying with us today and look forward to many more ventures."

It was Tessa's turn to roll her eyes while Wyatt chuckled. Her husband could be a goof.

He was, however, the best pilot she knew. And didn't mind living with an olive-skinned war goddess from the wrong side of the tracks—his words—even though it had caused him to be largely ostracized by his family for marrying "so far below his station."

One of these days, she'd go back to civilization to deal with his family, but right now, she had more pressing needs.

Outside, *Last Stand* settled onto the hot desert sands of *Orvan*.

Scene Two

Tessa noted that Fin had added a nice jacket that matched his green breeks. Blue, woolen socks that matched his shirt, then black, lace-up ankle boots. Pretty, which always struck her as exactly the wrong way to dress when committing armed robbery, but Fin was Fin, and nobody was going to tell him otherwise.

She'd gone with the tall boots today. Black leather cavalry style, with her tight, pinstriped pants tucked in. Brown today. Matching vest over a white dress shirt with a standing collar, though she was known to occasionally wear a tie when meeting with bankers.

It being hotter than shit outside the ship, she'd gone ahead and added a hijab to cover her head. Technically, she was supposed to wear one at all times around unrelated males, but that was pushing it. Tessa only wanted her hair under something today to keep the heat off her skull and sand out.

Behind Fin, Tessa's aunt Marusya emerged from the machine room and came down the rear steps. After the massive, terrible casualties of the wars that finally saw

Lorastir conquer Zaddinul, Maru was the only family Tessa had left, not counting the husband she'd gotten later. Similar, Marusya had lost a husband, four kids, and all her grandchildren.

Brutal. People talked about numbers, but until they had names, it didn't matter.

And Tessa had a lot of names.

Maru was wearing her usual semi-baggy pants with cargo pockets on the front and sides. Dark in spite of the heat outside. Lighter button-up shirt in a dove gray under a brown corset she wore to keep sparks and metal fragments from drawing blood.

Her long, black hair was up under an aviator's bonnet instead of a hijab, graying in stripes and white underneath.

Meeting the two of them on the street, one might think Marusya Kuznetsov was her mother. In blood instead of just spirit.

Like Fin, Maru was unarmed, carrying instead her little carpet bag of tools. Tessa and Wyatt were the heavies here.

Fortunately, their one regular passenger, Abigail, wasn't with them today, and had an alibi if Wyatt was correct and something had gone wrong. Tessa enjoyed having the woman around. A *Player*, Abigail Blackford was in great demand, as much for her singing and cooking as her conversations in the salon or the bedroom. Just having the woman as a long-term tenant of one of *Last Stand*'s shuttle bays lent the ship a patina of legitimacy and social acceptance they'd never normally have. Tin and only a patina, but better than nothing.

As she watched, Fin pulled heavy driving gloves and goggles from his pocket and got them on, before walking directly over to the cargo roller and hopping in. Hot and dry outside, so Tessa watched Aunt Maru join him and flip the windshield up from the forward deck, though she left the canvas top down. Better to have the gunners able to jump out the back at a moment's notice. Auntie rode up front with Fin, on his left.

Tessa and Wyatt took up their usual spots in the six-wheeled beast's cargo trunk. You could fit six back here if you weren't driving crazy, but she knew Fin, so Tessa laid her rifle down flat in the bed and made sure she had a good handhold. He might not stop if she got tossed out on her ass by some bump.

Best not to tempt it.

"Everybody ready?" Fin asked, though he didn't wait for an answer.

Instead, he triggered the remote control and the ramp deployed, letting the ugly morning heat in. Already thirty-five Celsius out there. Almanac said forty-two was average for a day like this, and she hadn't seen a single cloud in the sky to shade anything.

Fin rolled the electric cart down the ramp and started across the sands.

"You know where we're going?" Wyatt asked over the crunch of sand and hot breeze already puckering her skin.

"Actually, no," Fin yelled back. "Was just planning to drive around for a while ignoring directions until I found a convenience store where I could stop for cold beer and a potty break."

Tessa grinned. Wyatt grumbled. Auntie punched Fin lightly in the shoulder as the rest of them laughed.

It was a good crew, circumstances and civilization notwithstanding.

They came over a rise and Tessa got her first look at the target.

Huge. That was the first thought. Monstrous freighter down there in the sands like a dead, gray gator.

She hadn't gotten the details and didn't care enough to

ask, but the beast had suffered some sort of power failure during descent, managed to limp/glide this far, then crash soft enough to break the thing's spine but not scatter cargo all over the damned desert.

Small victories.

As it was, she could see where gear had failed to deploy in a few places. And others where the ship had still been moving forward and sideways enough to break off landing skids on impact.

But it had come down soft enough that nobody had died, wonder of wonders. Pilot must have been almost as good as her husband to manage that.

Being more than a thousand kilometers from the original target starport, however, it hadn't bothered anyone, and locals hadn't done more than fly over to note the location before calling the insurance company about a claim.

But it was a big beast. At least four hundred meters stem to stern. Maybe a third of that wide and a sixth tall in the middle. Big, damned sea turtle. She wondered idly as the cargo truck raced across the sands how many iterations of *Last Stand* a good cargo artist might fit in those nearly-endless bays.

Fortunately, she hadn't been hired to steal the whole thing. Just one box. Maybe a second for herself as a bonus, but that would have to wait until the one she was getting paid for was taken care of.

"I don't see a neon sign advertising cold beer," Fin announced, looking back over his shoulder at her. "Are we sure this is the right place?"

Tessa laughed. Everyone laughed. Fin smiled.

She nodded to Wyatt, though, as the two up front turned back forward. There might be guards down there.

Which was why they were armed.

Scene Three

Tessa was even more impressed as they got close. Most of this desert was hard stone and scrub, but the ship had managed to find a broad and long bowl of a valley, sand-filled, to crash in. Anywhere else and the ship probably would have disintegrated on impact.

Fin drove close to a hatch that would normally be up a short flight of steps. And horizontally true.

Today, it was about ten centimeters buried in blown sand on one side. She could work with that.

"Everybody out," Fin said, pausing.

Then she watched him expertly pivot the little cargo runner and back it into place. The box they needed might be small enough to come out a personnel hatch if they had rollers or a small repulsor scooter to move it.

Or she and Wyatt might end up lugging the damned thing. Tessa was stronger than she looked. Physically as well as emotionally.

That was only one of the reasons she'd survived the original **Last Stand**, back on *Vinoris*.

She put the dark thoughts out of her mind and focused

on the perimeter. Wyatt had the stern section watch, so she turned to the bow, invisible in the distance as barely enough breeze to lift dust had turned their arrival into a minor sandstorm.

Auntie got to work on the door. Ship still had power, according to the folks paying her to be here today. Not enough to fly, but they didn't need lifters. Air conditioning and doors would suffice. Hotter than the hell already awaiting all of them out here this morning.

Aunt Maru stood up from the door controls with a profanity that would have gotten Tessa's mouth washed out with soap when she was a kid.

"Wasn't even locked," Auntie said. "Wyatt here might have been able to open it."

"Hey!" Wyatt objected, but not too strenuously.

Auntie made his favorite cookies occasionally. When he'd been behaving.

Marusya hit a button and the door retracted into the wall with a grinding, tearing sound and the suggestion of motors burning out from the smell.

Not Tessa's problem.

"Wyatt, in," she ordered.

She had a better understanding of the interior than anybody else, having seen and memorized the original loading map when getting hired, but Wyatt was all about violence. Distilled and bottled up in that massive frame.

Ready to punch or shoot at the drop of a hat.

Not that Tessa wanted that sort of a reputation in the business, mind you. That sort of thing tended to get you an entirely different kind of job from the ones she preferred.

Better to be known as a cunning operator, sneaking in and out without casualties or significant property damage. Safer, too, as the big interstellar corporations weren't as likely to hire bounty hunters or mercenaries to come after you later.

Or at least not pay well enough to find quality professionals for the job.

Interior was dim. Raw metal walls sealed but not painted, so hammered-steel finish. Not enough lights, or maybe half were broken or turned off.

Whatever. Felt like breaking into a dungeon underground. Electricity was so cheap that most ships kept things at daylight all the time.

Wyatt got to the first intersection and correctly turned right. Man liked to pretend to be dumb. Tessa knew it was mostly a front to keep folks from asking him to be in charge.

He'd been a senior noncom for Lorastir during the war. She knew that much. Never made it to *Vinoris*, but that was fine. One of them with those memories was enough.

And she knew he'd been offered an officer's commission more than once and refused, from the way he talked about it. Didn't want the responsibilities.

She was also pretty sure he'd fragged a few officers in his time. Accidental friendly fire sort of thing.

Man had a problem with authority figures. Not her, but she also didn't push him. She let him be bigger and meaner and tougher than anybody else.

And Fin made him open pickle jars. And grab things down off top shelves her husband would have required a stepstool to reach.

Wyatt had given up grumbling about that once she'd reminded him that he couldn't have it both ways.

Today, he walked almost unerringly to the right cargo bay door.

"This one?" he asked, pointing with the hand not holding *Doomripper*.

"Next one, same side," Tessa replied.

She still wasn't sure he hadn't picked the wrong one on purpose.

You could never tell with Wyatt.

"Gonna need a roller," Fin announced, looking around. "Saw a sign for one plugged in forward from here."

"Wyatt, you and Auntie get this hatch open," Tessa decided. "We'll go get a hand truck."

Everyone nodded and she led them forward following helpful signs.

At one point, Fin grabbed her by the hip and slid her sideways into an alcove with a snicker.

"What?" she asked, looking down at the smile on his face.

"Well, we're all here stealing shit," he grinned. "Figured I should steal a kiss. Maybe a quick grope or two while we're at it. You know, criminal miscreants."

Tessa rolled her eyes, but leaned into the man and kissed him like she needed him to remember why he put up with her. And he did the same. She was certainly the crazier of the two of them. Fin never woke up from nightmares screaming.

A hand found her bottom and squeezed it as they necked.

She broke the kiss and smiled before they got too involved. Still in the middle of a job. Couldn't get too distracted.

He led and she followed. The hand truck was folded up in a closet, but it deployed with a button and Fin pushed it back.

Marusya had the cargo hold hatch open by the time they got there. Was inside somewhere while Wyatt kept watch, *Doomripper* sniffing the sound of their wheels approaching until he knew it was them.

He smiled and flipped his rifle's safety back on with a click.

"Is it in there?" she asked.

"I'm just hired muscle," he deflected. "Talk to the expert."

He meant Auntie. Anything not to have to be in charge. Not to have to make decisions.

She nodded and followed Fin into the side hold. Wyatt slid sideways into the gap by the hatch, so Tessa felt safe.

It was Wyatt's ass on the line, too, so that was a responsibility he took seriously.

Auntie was counting boxes and reading shipping stickers when they got close. She tapped a finger on the coffin-sized box at shoulder level.

"This one, I think?" she asked, turning to Tessa.

Tessa moved around Fin and his truck and read the manifest.

"Looks like," she said. She looked around but didn't see a crane. "Not sure how to get the top one off so we can steal this one."

"Nothing in it we want," Auntie Maru replied. "Label says machine parts for a bunch of communications and weather satellites. Headed to *Bernadette* when they wound up here. Probably just get melted down, since they aren't likely worth the cost to retrieve them."

Tessa looked at the manifest for that one. Heavy, at one hundred kilograms, but she didn't need to lift it. Just slide it off the stack and out of her way.

"Fin, do we have a crowbar or something?" she asked, looking around.

"Got one up here," Wyatt called quietly.

Tessa went and retrieved it from the little spot where Wyatt was standing, leaving her rifle leaned against another stack. Fin and Marusya had gotten all the lockdowns unlatched when she got back, so she slipped the meter-and-a-quarter bar into the gap and got underneath it.

Heavy, but she wasn't about to admit defeat. Too far from home. Lost a war and a life. Reduced to petty theft and armed robbery clear the hell out in the Periphery Sectors.

And she sure as hell couldn't go back to what used to be Zaddinul, before Lorastir took the whole Arles Region and turned it into their Empire. Under an asshole military genius who had been a revolutionary general a generation ago. Amarns Sigra, Emperor of Close Space, leaving the outer portions to places like Ergrove that had treaties and colonies making, growing, and mining stuff for the core worlds.

Tessa let that rage settle in her thighs and bottom as she stood up and levered that damned box off the top to fall with a hard, jarring thump in the next aisle.

Somebody else's problem to clean up. But didn't that describe most of the modern galaxy? Folks made messes, but didn't stop to clean them up afterwards?

Tessa left that one for the philosophers to argue. They had safe jobs teaching Lorastir kids linguistic games and never had to worry about mortgage payments or food. Not like real people.

She almost tossed the crowbar across the open space, then caught herself and leaned it up next to her rifle, trading one iron for the other.

Fin climbed up onto his roller and unhooked the latches as she watched, popping the top of the trunk open and whistling.

Curiosity got the better of her, so Tessa stepped up and looked in.

Iridium. Bars. Tiny ones, really. Forty millimeters wide, eighty long, and eighteen tall. Tool-grade stuff, though, so the purest, most valuable, since you got increasing percentages of platinum group metals in the mix as you worked your way down to Weapons-grade, Commercial-grade, and finally Coin-grade.

Each bar weighed 1.3 kilograms, and there were twenty-four of them in there.

A whole lot of money for the taking. Enough to hire her and her ship to slip in here and steal it.

Lots of people around these days, as Fin had said. Not enough jobs. Folks going hungry got desperate.

Like her.

"Close it up," she said.

Fin nodded and pulled the top down until the latches engaged. Tessa turned and looked around.

"Anything else small and valuable we might take?" she asked Auntie Maru.

"You and Fin get that loaded and I'll look around," the woman replied.

Tessa hadn't been willing to ask the broker for a manifest of things, even in this one cargo hold. He'd have charged her money for that information, when she was going to be here to look herself.

She rested her rifle out of the way again, twitchy about putting it down but needing both hands.

Hostile territory, ya know? Like them up on the Maburh Heights with their artillery, pouring shit down into the valley below, her and hers dug in like ticks next to the village of Clethorpe.

Them that survived.

Last Stand.

She and Fin locked eyes and moved to opposite ends of the coffin. Lighter than with a body inside, though she didn't want to think about that. Mostly awkward, because these things came in standard sizes, regardless of what you had to ship.

But her husband was tougher than he looked, too. He got under his end and lifted. She got her end up and moved around to line it up with the roller before setting it down and moving around to help him settle his end.

One box of iridium ingots, to go.

She grabbed her safety blanket rifle and looked around.

Marusya was down a bit, looking a mite indecisive. Tessa moved that way, Fin in her wake.

"Two options," Auntie grimaced. "Not sure which one yields a safer value."

"Safer?" Tessa asked.

"Things that don't have serial numbers some berk might track later," Auntie grinned.

"What do you have?" Tessa pressed.

"This one lists a crap ton of sample seeds," she said, slapping a box. "Looks like either a demonstration kit for a dealer somewhere, or some hobbyist white lady in a pretty mansion is taking up gardening because that's what people in her social circle do to show solidarity with us poor folk."

Tessa grimaced. She and Auntie were much darker-skinned. More olive. Auntie was talking about those pale, rich Lorastir ladies in their manor houses, having won the war and conquered all of the Arles Region. Or Ergrove women, masters of the Periphery because Lorastir hadn't wanted to expand beyond the Core. Folks whose greatest concern was getting their children into the best schools to turn them into future governors.

Or something.

"And the other?" Tessa asked.

A hand went out and tapped a different box. Short and squat.

"Business Analytical Engine," she said. "Tabulator version."

"A what?" Tessa was lost.

"Like the Personal Analytical Engines you have on the ship, only bigger," Maru explained. "Instead of just containing books to read or music to play, this has a full, mechanical keyboard that lets you do the data entry. Like a smaller version of the Household Analytical Engine fancy folks have for their recipe books, their contact lists, or their big music boxes."

"What would we do with one?"

Auntie shrugged.

"Probably sell it to a writer or a businesswoman," she replied. "You could run a small enterprise with such a thing and a little ingenuity."

"Got a business now," Tessa reminded her. "Or were you planning on striking out on your own?"

"Shit, no," Auntie laughed. "You and your man are stuck with me."

"That's good," Tessa said. "You two are all the family I have left. I take it your Business Analytical Engine is valuable?"

"Like the iridium, but only in the right hands," Auntie nodded. "The seeds can be grown or traded as is. Easier to make them vanish, especially down here in the shadows where we live."

"Agreed," Tessa decided. "We'll take the seeds. I have no idea what I'd do with a Tabulator."

"Start a revolution?" Fin asked.

She could tell that he was trying to make a joke, but it landed with a wet thud on her today. His face fell as he realized that.

"Sorry," he muttered, chagrined.

Fin was from Inleah. Scion of a long line of bankers,

though he'd always wanted to fly because, to hear him talk, his parents hardly ever even left their estate in the capital to visit the countryside, let alone get off the planet.

He'd wanted to see things.

And he'd missed the war. Inleah had sold guns and shit to anyone with money to buy, but maintained a hard neutrality. Amoral, even.

He'd never even been shot at until he married her.

Tessa had seen the war from the inside. From the *Last Stand* at *Vinoris*.

She nodded that it was okay. Not all of his jokes were funny, but most of them were.

She wasn't a revolutionary. That had been burned out of her in the battle. And the camps afterwards, when their Lorastir captors hadn't really cared if the few individuals who had managed to surrender lived or not.

A woman did what she had to do to survive that sort of thing.

Tessa drew a breath and kept her own counsel. Fin meant well.

A voice at the main hatch interrupted everything.

"What's going on here?"

Scene Four

Tessa turned, automatically aiming her rifle at the voice. Nobody she knew, and she and hers were in the middle of committing all manner of unattractive felonies.

Fellow stood in the open hatchway of the cargo hold, dark suit and a black, felt derby on his head. Looked tall, but Tessa wasn't close enough to tell from over here. About half the men she met were shorter than she was.

He had a flashlight in his hands, but no gun that she could see. Which was good, because a ghost materialized out of the shadows and *Brunhilde*'s barrel appeared right there in the corner of his eyes where the man could turn and flinch away with a shocked profanity generally unfit for mixed company.

"Man's unarmed," Tessa said, starting that direction with an intent stride.

And her own rifle pointed at him.

"We all get up in the morning and make stupid decisions," Wyatt replied in a dry, heavy voice. The one he practiced.

Tessa needed to head that off. Killing a man in self-defense was one thing. Shooting him like a rabid dog something else.

"Anybody with you?" Tessa demanded as she got close.

The fellow's hands were up and his flashlight rolling around on the floor nearby, casting weird shadows. His face was pure rage at being surprised by Wyatt.

"No," he snarled. "Just me."

His lip curled when he got a good look at her. The hijab probably didn't help. He was seeing how much darker her skin was than his. Ergrove folks tended to be so pale that they turned pink in the sun. Even tanned, they were a different shade.

He wanted to speak that word that was on the tip of his tongue. The one those lovely rich pale folks used to describe her kind. Tessa wasn't sure if she would cold-cock him with her rifle butt or shoot him in the belly if he did, though.

Fellow developed smarts before anyone had to discover that answer.

Wyatt had seen it, too. His eyes could etch diamond right now. Wasn't the sort of thing you normally expected from a brute like Wyatt Nakada, but he'd served with her crew for two years, so he didn't have that sort of racism in him. Obviously didn't like it in anyone else.

Before Tessa could react, Wyatt stepped forward and chopped the man on the side of the neck with *Brunhilde* and a nasty crack of steel on flesh.

Man went down like a sack of potatoes.

Tessa wanted to be angry with Wyatt. Wasn't in her. He'd found his place in life, and didn't want anyone else pissing her off.

If she was in jail, he'd have to go find a real job or something.

Tessa knelt and looked at the fellow. Quickly rifled his pockets. Found his ID wallet and flipped it open.

Masterson Galactic Investigations. She grimaced and flashed it to Wyatt, just so he knew who he'd hit.

Rough folk. Not strike breakers, but the folks who you hired to break a strike by hiring the thugs and scab pilots you might need. Weren't bounty hunters, either, but the folks you'd hire for taking care of such a thing.

Brokers. Just outside the law, but only because the law didn't extend as far as folks with money might need it to.

At least this one was a simple Operative, and not a Detective or an Inspector. Punk, for all he looked to be in his mid-thirties. Older than Tessa by a ways. Older than Fin. Waxed handlebar mustache she'd missed from the way the shadows had played across his face, but that seemed perfect for the character he'd been playing.

Tessa rooted around until she found his handcuffs, then located at least one key. Man probably had several others hidden about his person. Masterson Ops were like that.

She cuffed his right wrist, then hooked the other to a nearby case. Not enough to do more than hold him for a while, since all she needed to do was get away later.

Tessa looked up and noted that Fin and Auntie had the roller close. It could even slip down this aisle without having to drive over the man's foot. Fin might do that anyway, but that was a different conversation.

"We got everything we need?" Tessa asked the other three.

"We want his badge?" Wyatt asked with a smirk.

"Don't see why," Tessa countered.

Impersonating a Masterson Op was a guaranteed easy way to have them send angry folks after you later. Some scoundrels did that anyway, but they were all charlatans vanishing into con job roles on the fly anyway.

Not a headache she needed.

"Just wondering," Wyatt nodded, turning to step to the door with guns pointed both ways as his head went back and forth.

Anybody but Wyatt, and that would look comical. She'd watched him shoot two people at opposite ends of a hall that way.

Tessa dropped the handcuff key just far enough out of reach that the man would need a little flexibility to get to it. Hadn't had a comm of any kind on him, so he wasn't calling for backup. She supposed a smart Op might have checked in when he heard sounds, but she was already on a clock ticking down in her head and moving quickly to avoid the law.

Or anybody else.

"Let's go," she ordered, nodding Wyatt into motion.

Tessa trailed, looking back regular-like, but the Op hadn't had anything but a sap on him, so he wasn't a threat now, except as he might have friends.

"Pay attention for trouble at the main hatch," she reminded Wyatt as they moved that way.

"Looking forward to it," he replied.

She supposed he was, being Wyatt and all.

Tessa just needed to get out of here, back to the ship, and off the planet to where they could meet with their own broker and get paid for all these shenanigans.

A day in the life of a businesswoman.

Scene Five

TESSA SENT FIN FORWARD AND UP TO HIS COCKPIT TO GET them gone. Auntie Maru followed halfway *en route* to her machines. That left her and Wyatt to deal with the cargo once she got the rear cargo ramp up and locked.

"Shoulda let me shoot him," Wyatt muttered, just quiet enough that she could ignore it if she chose.

He knew where the lines were, after a few ugly incidents along the way to draw them.

"Wouldn't have solved anything," she said. "As is, we did enough to piss the Masterson Agency off. Doubt we've got big game hunters in our future, but we'll burn that bridge when we get there."

He grunted and followed as she moved to a sidewall and started fiddling with a panel. It stuck a lot, which was actually better, since there was less chance of a random passenger accidentally discovering that it moved.

Eventually, it opened, and they slid the iridium inside.

"What about the other one?" he asked.

"Want to haul it to the coffin wall," Tessa replied, starting to close it up. "We ain't hauling any travelers right now, so we can stuff it in one of them while we deal with Raven."

"Don't want him knowing we stole a bunch of seeds?"

"Don't want him knowing we took anything," Tessa countered. "He hired us for the iridium. The rest is profit. Especially seeds. You know how valuable some of those will be shipboard. Nobody likes eating meal packs, but you do what you gotta if you can't afford better. Fresh stuff does wonders for the mind as well as the body."

"Fin has enough pickles," Wyatt grumbled.

Tessa laughed out loud.

"Fin never has enough pickles," she replied mirthfully. "If I'd let him, he'd turn one of the empty cabins into a full-on hydroponics lab to experiment with cucumbers. I'd have to land on some planet with a salt pan on the surface and let him load a ton or two, then find somebody growing dill in commercial amounts."

"Something ain't right with that boy," Wyatt shook his head.

Tessa grinned.

"He married me," she said. "That should have been your first clue."

That, at least, got a grin out of the big hunk of muscle and attitude problem. He moved to the other end of the seed box and they lifted.

Forward past the cargo elevator to the second deck, then past the rear set of cabins for paying customers that Tessa hadn't been desperate enough to allow. Wyatt bunked back here, with her and Fin sharing a cabin forward and Marusya across from them.

Tessa didn't think that either of those two might have snuck to the other's cabin some night, but she also didn't ask. Wyatt was big and white and thirty-five, while Auntie Maru was small and dark and fifty-seven.

Don't want to know. Don't share, thank you.

Past Wyatt's cabin there were two sets of coffin walls, one down each side of the hallway. Three bays tall and three wide, each 1.2m square on the front, and 2.4m deep. Eighteen spaces if she had to haul a lot of folks in an emergency. More if you doubled up, but that wouldn't be the least bit comfortable to sleep for any couple she knew.

No way to haul that many people for long anyway, as she rarely had enough food for all those hungry mouths and life support would be sucking hind tit in a hurry trying to keep up with foul air.

"We care which one?" Wyatt asked.

"Not on your side, unless you want Auntie waking you up when she gets in to inventory it," Tessa replied.

He nodded and opened the bottommost, aftmost, starboard-side coffin. They set the box down and she watched him crawl into the opening. Moving the folded up blanket out of the way instead of squishing it under the box.

Wyatt had weird habits he'd picked up from somewhere. Keeping a ship spotless happened to be the one she appreciated the most. Even dirty dishes didn't last long in the sink after dinner if he didn't have anything requiring his mind.

They made a good crew.

He grunted and slid out. Tessa turned the box and slid it home like a cartridge in the barrel.

"Now what?" he asked as they stood up.

"Now, we go talk to Raven about getting paid," Tessa nodded.

Another day in the business of crime.

Scene Six

Tessa was up on the flight deck with Fin when they came out of hyperspace. Weren't even that far off with this jump, but that was Fin's touch. Nobody else she'd ever known could lock in the inertial system with such precision and delicacy. He had a gift for things like that.

Other folks flying, they aimed and prayed. Kind of like having a firefight in a dark warehouse. Not that she'd ever done that, either.

But they were above *Alfann* and not even that far out.

"Kinda looking forward to maybe finding a hotel with nice sheets and a view for a couple of days," Fin offered. "Get room service and take you to bed, except when we're sitting on a balcony drinking tea, wearing nothing but sheets we've torn off the mattress."

She glanced over and grinned. Sandy blond hair a little too long. Precisely trimmed mustache and Van Dyke. He even *looked* like a banker, but a friendly kind, if there was such a critter.

Tessa was across in the co-pilot seat, not that she

hardly ever flew *Last Stand*, but it let her spend time with her husband. She brought the comm live and started to send a note to Raven, but the inbound message queue was filling quicker than normal and had way too many priority messages popping up.

She paused with a hand on the microphone and put it back.

"Lots of traffic," she said, moving to clear all the junk mail.

Unfortunately, just deleting everything wasn't an option. Too many folks in her line of work couldn't transmit messages in the clear, so they had to code things.

"Shit," she said abruptly.

"Troubles, beautiful?" Fin asked.

She read the message again, just to make sure she'd gotten the gist of it the first time.

"Authorities picked up Raven," she said, just loud enough to hear.

"That's not good," Fin replied. "We know why?"

"Might be that they just rounded up the usual suspects," she offered weakly. "But even that's questionable."

"They looking for us?" he pressed.

"No way that they could have gotten a message from *Orvan* to *Alfann* ahead of us," she said. "Not this quickly. Same time, I'm not sure what our next steps should be, on account of us hauling a lot of stolen iridium."

"Is it marked?" he asked. "Like serial numbers and all that?"

"No, but that kind of bar stock isn't common," she replied. "Once folks know it got stolen, they'll start putting the pieces together. We either have to carry it around for a year or dump it quick on someone that can hide it instead."

"Well, we're at *Alfann*," Fin said. "There ought to be all manner of types even more disreputable than us to handle that, right?"

"Normally, yes," she grimaced. "I got notes here that suggest a major sweep. Not just Raven, but a whole bunch of others."

"Somebody decided to clean up *Alfann*?" Fin asked, astonished. "Actually tried?"

She felt the astonishment as well.

"It's still *Alfann*," she reminded her husband. "If the economy of the Periphery worked in the first place, they wouldn't need smugglers. If they take all the dealers out of the equation, a lot of the planet probably falls apart in a hurry and they start having plagues and starvation."

He nodded rather than answer that. Inleah had always been a wealthy, open society. Lots of money, so crime was the genteel sort. Bankers robbing other bankers. Grifters running elaborate con jobs on tycoons.

Poor people weren't worth robbing.

"Orders?" he asked, reminding her that she was in charge and he was just a kept man. Like he liked it.

"Set us down in Weinsefeld Port like we originally planned," Tessa replied. "But keep things quiet for now while I make some inquiries."

"How are we doing for money?" he asked as she rose from the co-pilot chair.

"Not well enough that I want to haul that iridium any farther than I have to," she replied. "Not bad enough that I'm desperate. Yet."

"Auntie Maru wanted me to remind you that we're behind on the maintenance cycle," Fin nodded as she crossed and kissed his forehead.

"Yeah," she said. "I know."

She turned and descended the steps to the main deck. Her notes on *Alfann* were hidden in her cabin and she needed to review them.

If Raven was out of the picture, she needed a new broker somewhere.

Scene Seven

Tessa looked around Weinsefeld Docks. Mid-afternoon. Fall hemisphere. Damp streets but the rain had moved by before *Last Stand* had landed, leaving everything in that brief moment of beautiful crisp air you got when the drizzle knocked down the smell of desperation and cooking grease.

Almost smelled like Weinsefeld City right now, where all the money was, at the other end of the tram.

She didn't need the tram. Wasn't going to meet folks with money. No bankers in her future, other than the cute scion of financiers she'd run away with and married.

The four of them were down on the cargo deck with the main hatch open. The Docks themselves were all in a line for smaller ships like hers. Big cargo ships were farther out, each in their own pit with services handy. Here, you were kind of on your own.

"We need a better cover story," Auntie Maru said out of the blue.

"Suggestions?" Tessa asked. Maybe a bit testy. "I won't know anything about anything until I get into the

Strip and talk to folks. Play it casual for now and pretend like this was a deadhead run, instead of us smuggling, okay?"

"We know when Abigail is due back?" Wyatt asked.

No interest in his voice about the woman. Nor feigned indifference. He'd probably propositioned her once, been shot down, and gone on with his life. Wyatt wasn't one to brood on women. Another reason she put up with him.

"Tonight or early tomorrow morning," Fin replied. "She always keeps space at the back of her schedule to extend a client at the last minute."

Tessa nodded.

Abigail Blackford was a Player. They existed outside the usual social strata of society, able to mix freely with the cream as well as the scum. At first, Tessa had thought that they were extremely expensive prostitutes. Or maybe courtesans, but Abigail had set her to right.

Players were social companions. Actors. Bards. Entertainers. Raconteurs. Beauty wasn't even necessary, because they seduced you with wit and manners, male or female. And they could cook.

Maybe sex was on the menu. Maybe not. As Abigail had told her at one point, "If I wanted to be nothing more than a wife or mistress, I wouldn't have gone to school for a decade."

Having her as a long-term tenant meant that *Last Stand* always had a little money coming in, which went a long ways when jobs were few and far between.

Or went wrong and you were left holding the bag.

Tessa turned to Fin and Auntie.

"You two hold down the fort," she said. "Wyatt and I will head into town and see what we can find out and be back for dinner. Hopefully, we'll have news at that point, and Abigail will be home early if we need to depart in a rush."

"What about hauling passengers?" Maru asked.

"We don't know where we're going next," she reminded Auntie.

"Not everyone has to have a destination," Marusya countered. "Some folks just want a ride."

"If they have enough money for a cabin and don't care about itinerary," Tessa decided. "Nobody for the coffins on this run, since we don't want anyone knowing about the seeds."

Auntie Maru nodded.

"Guns?" Wyatt asked expectantly when she turned to him.

"Sidearms only," she said. "We're trying to look innocent here."

"You can't always finesse the situation, boss," he replied flatly. "Sometimes, ya gotta blow shit up."

"That's why I'm taking you with me into the Docks, Wyatt," she grinned. "Maybe you'll get lucky and someone will start a bar brawl."

His eyes lit up like a kid in a candy store.

"Ya think?"

"We'll see," she said.

She turned to kiss Fin on the mouth and Auntie on the cheek. She and Wyatt were armed, as were the rougher third of the Docks crowd on any given day. Few honest folks about, though she supposed that the ratio had gone up with Raven and a lot of his ilk arrested.

Not that a place like Weinsefeld Docks could be cleaned up that quickly. If at all. All that would come of it was a new batch of grifters and predators taking over. Ergrove didn't want their various colonies in the Periphery becoming too successful and wealthy. Might make Lorastir nervous. Or jealous enough to maybe start building starships again.

Uneasy peace back in the Arles Region. Inleah and others remained studiously neutral. Ergrove had a massive fleet that could keep Lorastir at bay, but no real army, nor any great interest in building one.

Zaddinul had been the biggest rival to Lorastir, once then-Revolutionary General Sigra had captured Altenfeld and rolled up all those various principalities and duchies into a single place. Later, as Emperor, he'd gone ahead and finished off Zaddinul.

As a result, there were a lot of darker faces like hers on the Periphery. Ergrove might own the planets, but they didn't have the people to develop them. Nor did they want to create their own rivals later, so they let places run wild and rough. Race issues on top of culture and accent went a long ways towards making sure nobody could unify things out here and maybe decide to break away from Ergrove and start their own place.

Ergrove Port Authorities were the type to hire Masterson Operatives to do things, since sometimes they didn't have the law on their side.

Tessa's glower at the universe maintained a bubble around her as she walked out of the Dock itself and down onto the Strip. Part of that was Wyatt beside her, scowling at anyone and everyone and hoping somebody was dumb enough to try to mug him in broad daylight.

There were dumber ways to die, but he liked to remind you that folks got up and made dumb decisions every morning. Picking a fight with an angry giant was certainly up there.

They got to Three Rocks Tavern pretty quickly. It had been a pawn shop once, that somehow managed to go out of business but kept the sign. Supposedly, it represented three gold coins, back when gold was used for currency instead of jewelry.

Dewey was behind the bar this afternoon. He was a little guy, but only physically. Tessa had seen him pull out a length of metal pipe and use it on a drunk Wyatt's size without any hesitation. Then drag the silly git out the front door by himself.

She moved to an empty spot at the bar and leaned against the old, stained wood.

"What'll it be, *stranger*?" Dewey asked in a hard, calculating voice.

Tessa started to say something tart to the man, but caught her tongue. Dewey was a fixture of the Docks. The Tavern was on its fourth owner, near as she could figure, and he'd worked for three of them. He knew everyone that passed through.

Last time, he'd had a glass of rum for her and one of those cute, fruity drinks that came with paper umbrellas in nicer establishments that Wyatt liked on the bar before she'd even spoken.

She fixed him with a hard glare and caught the recognition in his eyes, before they slid off and located someone across the room. Dewey had a polished steel mirror on the barback behind him, so she followed his eyes.

Hard men in black over in a corner. Not uniforms, but not far off. Mercenaries, which covered a broad multitude of sins in a place like Weinsefeld Docks.

"Rum," she said over the low noise of customers. "Something cute and fruity for my friend here. Preferably with an umbrella in it."

"Out of umbrellas this year," he replied idly as his hands went to work and his eyes came back to her. "Been kinda rough around here lately."

She nodded and held all her questions inside. Dewey would know who was replacing a guy like Raven. Or a whole cast of brokers if the authorities had decided to do something.

They could have waited a week. Then she'd be off somewhere else and not hauling forty kilograms of stolen, Tool-grade iridium around, waiting for someone to arrest her.

"New in town?" he asked as he set down a pair of glasses. Wyatt's even had ice and a pair of sweetened cherries, like he liked it.

"Just flew in today," Tessa nodded, slipping a coin across the counter.

More than two drinks and a tip worth. It vanished under a hand then into the aether before anybody noted the face value.

"New day on *Alfann*," Dewey said, eyes on a horizon somewhere in a way that might have fooled the average fool.

"They cleaning up the planet?" she asked.

"Maybe trying to," he shrugged. "Not sure it's likely to happen."

Beside her, Wyatt had his glass in hand and had turned around to watch the room. Maybe eyeballing folks and hoping someone would take offense and say something.

Wyatt could be like that. She tapped him in the hip with an elbow, kind of like you might pull the reins on a horse when he got to feeling frisky. Wyatt relaxed.

Last thing she needed right now was to be picked up by the authorities for being involved in a brawl. Even in a place like Three Rocks.

"Hoping it's not the end of an era around here," Dewey offered vaguely. "Might end up having to go someplace like *Newhall*. Maybe see if my cousin Bao Li has work.

Can't see a place like this surviving as a neighborhood bar where they expect me to wear a tie or something."

Tessa nodded to the man and he moved off to fill glasses down the line.

She turned around to look at the clientele and imagined all the accumulated junk on the shelves being replaced by ferns or something. Maybe a carpet over the raw concrete floor. Putting in real tables instead of steel ones bolted down so nobody could use them in a fight.

The four mercenaries in the corner were watching her, but not with the sorts of aggressiveness that put her hand on the pommel of her revolver.

She still drank left-handed in case she needed to get to it quickly. Wyatt was the same way.

He slurped his frilliness and watched.

Crowd in here felt different from last time they'd been in, a week or so ago after talking to Raven and getting a contract from the man. Harder in some ways, softer in others.

Brokers being gone opened space. Some of it was filled with simple folk just trying to have a quiet drink on a quiet afternoon. Some of it, like those four in black, looked to be predators sniffing to see if they could move in and take over.

Tessa drank and considered Dewey's words. He didn't have a cousin on *Newhall*. Well, unless you considered that they were all cousins of a sort. Service industry types finding things for folks. In Dewey's case, a little alcohol and relaxation.

That was his way of passing along a message, and doing it in such a way that most folks wouldn't understand. But then, he'd treated her like a stranger, instead of a friendly regular who came in when dealing with a true regular like Raven.

Bao Li wasn't someone Tessa had worked with all that much. Older woman. Middle-aged, give or take, somewhere between Tessa and Auntie Maru.

Newhall wasn't as big or troublesome as *Alfann* got. That was good and bad. Smaller market for goods. Smaller cast of folks serving those needs.

Things might be about to get a mite interesting if folks from *Alfann* started showing up looking for work. And bringing their troubles with them.

Beside her, Wyatt was chewing ice, having finished his drink. Probably saving the cherries.

Not a man given to the finer things in life. Nor accustomed to presenting with manners. Too much like work. Too much like being an officer.

She hadn't been either, but by that point, they'd been grabbing folks like her off the street to fill out the fading bits of their army. They'd handed her a rifle and expected her to die like the rest ended up doing.

Something like ninety percent casualties, if the reports were to be believed.

Tessa had always assumed those numbers were low.

Those four over there looked of an age to have been there, seven years ago. Darker than Ergrove. Lighter than most of Zaddinul, not counting the aristocrats who'd been tossed out on their asses after the war.

The serfs ended up with new masters. Nothing else much had changed.

When you're poor, you're a nobody.

Worse, ethnically, she and Auntie were *Vlikine*. One of the few of her kind that Zaddinul hadn't wiped out before the war started, though they'd been trying.

In some weird way, Emperor Sigra invading had saved her. Had caused the Zaddinul government to stop oppressing her kin, mostly because they were too busy losing wars elsewhere to finish the *Vlikine* off.

One of the mercs was looking at her like he recognized her. Might be simply staring at her face.

Fin always talked about her cheekbones, so incredibly wide and flat, framing a thin nose and full lips. Strong jaw, soft chin. Dark, wideset eyes and straight black hair. Olive skin.

Classically beautiful, even in Lorastir, if she'd been a brunette with pink skin. Zaddinul never got past her tribe to see her as anything but a problem to be dealt with.

She fixed the merc staring at her with a hard eye, daring him to start something when she was already cranky and Wyatt looking for a rumble.

The man lowered his eyes after a moment and Tessa shot the rest of her rum, reaching back to rest it on the bar without turning to look.

Wyatt popped both cherries in his mouth and did the same. His head was on a pivot as she walked to the front door, her turning immediately right and breaking into a trot that had the taller man catching up.

She went down half a block, then ducked into a rug dealer, Wyatt fast on her heels.

The shop keeper started to say something, but she shushed him and slid into a spot where she was largely invisible from the street but able to see back the way she'd come. Wyatt headed deeper into the shop.

A few moments later, the four mercenaries appeared, looking around but not seeing her. They hadn't played this game before. Tessa had.

They put their heads together for a long moment, then headed the other direction. The way she'd come originally. Hopefully, Fin was sharp enough to keep the ship buttoned up right now, since they weren't dealing with cargo immediately. Those four looked like the type that might bum rush it.

Then they'd have to deal with an angry Marusya. Folks would get hurt if that happened.

Tessa turned back to see Wyatt rifling through the rugs in the corner, asking the keeper questions. She held a civil tongue and joined him, reasonably confident that the watchers were lost for the moment.

So she got to watch Wyatt haggle the price down to a pretty good deal for a meter-by-two rug in blue with black and green patterns worked in. He paid and slung the roll over his shoulder like a body.

Tessa fought the urge to roll her eyes. You never knew what Wyatt Nakada was up to. In some ways, he came across as a simple man, violent and ruthless. Then he drank things with umbrellas and bought pretty rugs for himself.

But it was his money. She paid him reasonably well, though he was still on the hook for his own ammunition these days. Nobody starved, and he occasionally did things like this.

"Those four punks in black come looking for us?" he asked as they made it back into the street.

She turned right and set out on a different path home.

How he'd known, Tessa wasn't sure, other than the potential for violence.

"They did," she acknowledged. "Anybody you know?"

"Nope, but they served in Lorastir at one point," he said, sliding adroitly past folks in spite of his mass and that rug. "Infantry, like you. It's in the way they move. And their eyes."

He'd also been in the Lorastir army, but didn't talk about the things he'd done. Or the places he'd been.

She didn't ask.

It was enough that he occasionally turned out to be sharper and smarter than most people gave him credit for. He had to be relaxed to make sharp comments like that.

Right now, she needed to get back to her ship. And do it quietlike, since there were some bad men running around with far too great an apprehension about her business.

Lots of things going on about *Alfann* and the Docks.

Might already be time to be moving on.

Scene Eight

Tessa had found a spot near the ship but not out in the open. Wyatt had slipped into an alley as the afternoon shadows got longer, telling her he'd scout and return in a bit.

Wyatt did that well, so she watched. None of those four were in evidence, but that didn't mean anything. She was pretty well hidden herself right now.

Fin was on the street outside the main hatch, talking to a woman Tessa didn't know. Older, maybe Maru's age of late fifties. Much heavier, though she moved with smooth grace. Hair fully gray and short, barely longer than a banker or lawyer might wear it. Not like Tessa's down and occasionally braided.

Fin and the stranger were talking. Seemed casual and friendly. Auntie was nowhere to be seen, but that didn't mean anything. Fin was born to bankers, so dealing and schmoozing were second nature when he needed to turn on the charm.

They shook hands after a moment and the heavy woman nodded, turning and walking away without glancing back. Wyatt appeared around the far corner of the ship a few moments later, from a spot she didn't think you could get to without crossing a half-empty street and being seen.

But it was Wyatt. He walked right up and likely scared Fin half to death, coming up behind him. They talked briefly, then both looked her direction. Wyatt made a gesture with his right hand that it was safe, so Tessa emerged from her alley and slid along the side of the building, trying not to skulk as she did.

Wyatt was all grins when she got close, then immediately walked into the ship, so everything must be hunky-dory with him, rug roll over his shoulder.

Whether that meant no mercenaries, or he'd snuck up on the group and beaten them all up by himself, wasn't the sort of thing you asked on an open street, so she kissed her husband.

"Anything good?" she asked.

"Possible traveler looking for a cabin," he said, noting the look in her eyes and the way Wyatt had walked. "Didn't make any promises until you could meet her. We're supposed to join her for dinner in a few hours, down the street where she's currently staying."

"Saw her as I was watching the ship," Tessa nodded. "Anything strike you odd about the woman?"

"Define odd," he smiled. "I married you, *Last Stand*, and Auntie Maru. Plus Wyatt. Not sure I have a solid grasp of what *normal* might be like."

She grinned. They always said to never marry somebody crazier than you, but Fin was the sane one here.

"We saw a group of four guys in town," she said in a quieter voice, keeping an eye on the street.

Too early in the day for folks headed home from work or out to dinner. Late enough that they might be sneaking off to have a drink before going home. Pedestrian traffic was at a lull, but Wyatt had indicated that nobody was watching the ship. And gone inside, though that might just be so he could grab *Doomripper* if he needed to.

"Trouble?" Fin asked.

"Mercenaries of some sort," she replied. "Dewey pretended like he'd never met me before, so the place was crawling with folks he didn't trust. Suggested we head to *Newhall* and talk to Bao Li since Raven was out of the picture, at least for a while."

"Don't know that name." Fin's brow furrowed. "We trust it?"

"I dealt with her a few times, back when I first came to the Hawkswold Sector," Tessa said. "Before I met this cute flyboy who swept me off my feet."

"I seem to remember that you bought me a drink first," he grinned up at her. "So maybe I'm just an innocent victim of your feminine wiles?"

"You keep right on telling yourself that," Tessa teased.

"That's my story and I'm sticking to it," he nodded. "Now what?"

"Let's lock up then," Tessa said. "We'll talk to your potential traveler. What's her name?"

"Laney Coburn," he replied.

"We'll meet Coburn and see what she's about," Tessa said. "Then hopefully Abigail's home tonight and we can maybe slip off while everyone is asleep."

"*Alfann* suddenly too hot to stay around?" he asked.

"I got a bad feeling, Fin," she said.

Scene Nine

Tessa had put Wyatt on watch and dragged her husband back to their cabin for a little light fooling around. Not enough that either of them needed a shower afterwards, but a relaxing hour or so.

As a result, she was in a much better frame of mind as evening started sneaking over the horizon of old ships and worn buildings visible from *Last Stand*'s bridge.

Wyatt joined them, with Marusya trailing him up the steps.

"I got take-out being delivered in a few minutes," he announced. "Enough for the two of us."

Auntie looked a little surprised at that, but shrugged. She enjoyed cooking, but also understood where the big man's head was right now.

"When you and Fin head out, I'll be at the bar next door, by the front," he continued in a serious tone. "If there's trouble, just throw a chair through one of the front windows and I'll come running."

"Can't do that anymore," Maru replied. "They put in unbreakable ones after last time. Remember?"

"Oh, shit, that's right," he snapped his fingers. "Should I be inside, maybe at the bar?"

"They're likely to have you arrested on sight, Wyatt," Fin reminded the man. "You were that one that broke all the windows in the first place."

"Fellow had it coming," Wyatt said defensively, kind of scrunching himself down, which looked rather comical, as big as he was.

"Water under the bridge," Tessa told him. "I'll take a short-range transmitter. You keep an earpiece listening. Auntie, if there's trouble, being warm on all your generators gives us five minutes head start. We heard from Abigail?"

"Due before midnight," Wyatt said. "Didn't get the impression that her last client was going to convince her to drag out goodbyes."

Players. Entertainers, but Abigail didn't have a fixed circuit she worked. Instead, the woman traveled world to world wherever *Last Stand*'s deliveries took them, making herself available at any stop, if you could afford her price for an evening's entertainment. Or a night's.

Tessa didn't understand it. Or Abigail. Woman had money, looks, family, connections, and brains. And becoming a certified Player took a decade of expensive training, so it wasn't the sort of thing you undertook lightly.

Still, she seemed happy. And appeared to enjoy traveling with the crew of misfits that made up *Last Stand*.

"We're going to treat this like a normal business meeting," Tessa announced. "Wyatt will be armed nearby. Maru will have the engines ready for immediate takeoff if we have to run like that one time. I'll be armed, because they might remember that you still work for me, Wyatt."

"Another Tuesday night on the Docks," Fin noted dryly.

Tessa couldn't argue that point with the man. In some of the joints up and down the Strip, a good night was one where nobody got stabbed in the bathroom.

She had changed into a nicer shirt, but still put on the layer of armor underneath. She didn't have as much chest as Abigail, but a layer of bulletproof cloth helped hold everything in place nicely.

And she had been shot more than once on *Alfann*.

They headed aft when Wyatt's food arrived, all sitting in the dining hall as he and Auntie ate stir-fry. Looking around, it was almost time to harvest more oregano and mint from various pots and hydroponics. Spinach, kale, and mustard got trimmed regularly to add greens to meals. And the pepper plant was starting a fresh crop, just turned the first bit of orange on the oldest few.

Tomorrow's issue. Tonight, she needed to meet a potential customer and see if she liked the woman enough to let her fly with them. Usually, not as big a problem, but those four mercenaries had been trouble just waiting to happen, and Tessa wasn't sure if this Laney Coburn was connected or not.

Wyatt went first. Needed time to scout things in the neighborhood. She was fine with that, because the only people he would hurt had it coming. At least to hear him explain it.

He'd never led her astray on the topic.

Weather outside had dropped cooler as the evening had progressed, like it did in the fall at Weinsefeld, so she'd added a brown long coat. Fin was wearing a nicer outfit than the restaurant deserved, but it had nothing to do with them.

He held out an elbow and she took it, looking like two newlyweds out on a promenade. Three years married, but Auntie Marusya still complained about how cute they were in public, holding hands and giggling.

Foot traffic had picked back up as they emerged into twilight, but Wyatt had called things clear. She and Fin walked down the middle of the street, jostled occasionally, but that was simply folks in a hurry to get somewhere. Clouds were slowly building overhead, so maybe they worried about rain.

The restaurant was socially a step up from Three Rocks Tavern, but that wasn't a high bar to clear. Sailors and crew from ships along the Docks, plus locals who served them and preyed on them.

She recognized the big woman sitting in a corner table as they entered and got waved over. Tessa let Fin lead and trailed him, watching the rest of the crowd. Wyatt knew who the mercenaries were, and none were visible, but that didn't mean anything at all.

"Laney Coburn, my wife and boss, Tessa Sladek," Fin introduced them as she got close.

Coburn rose from her chair with smooth grace. Tall woman. Maybe one hundred and seventy-five centimeters to Tessa's one eighty-three.

Much bigger and bulkier though. Tessa had muscles that put her usual weight at about seventy-five kilograms. Coburn was easily above ninety. And it wasn't a pot belly hanging over her belt. Broad shoulders that didn't pinch in at all for a waist, then built back up to powerful thighs. Arms like Tessa had thighs. Thighs like tree trunks.

Dressed in a white, folded collar shirt with an open neck and slate gray slacks. A black vest that buttoned like a bib shirt, the bottom-most button about over her belly button, then they worked up towards her right shoulder in a slight curve rather than up the center of her chest, as might be considered traditional.

Odd, but fashionable. Exotic, without saying much of anything.

Face said Zaddinul. Darker than Lorastir, though not as far down into olive as Tessa. But she had been considered dark among those folks.

Tessa shook the woman's hand. Dry. Rough skin with the kind of callouses you got from doing hard labor with them.

The table was round and had four chairs. Fin sat across from Coburn, while Tessa took the other side of the corner looking out, as the woman had a perfect view of the front door and those windows that could probably stop bullets these days.

Wyatt had been a bit excessive when he put that one fellow through one. But he had had it coming.

They made small talk. Nothing consequential. Waitress came and took their order. Nobody Tessa knew, but folks swapped around jobs on the Strip fairly regular-like. Got tired of the same boss and the same clients.

That was one of the reasons why Tessa preferred to fly. Always something different.

Tessa studied Coburn as they were alone. Woman had a hard, dangerous air about her.

"What did you do during the war?" she asked the older woman.

Tessa had only been part of it at the very end, long after the war itself had mostly fizzled out when Zaddinul's capital at *Baramunz* fell to Lorastir troops. Other worlds had surrendered voluntarily for the most part, but a few had refused to let the fight go.

Tessa had ended up being recruited by an armed posse on *Vinoris*, like it or not.

Coburn studied her now, as if seeing the *Last Stand* itself in Tessa's eyes. That battle was never far from the surface.

And how someone talked about the war, which had ended twelve years ago at *Baramunz* or seven at *Vinoris*, said a lot about how they saw themselves. Especially clear out here on the Periphery in Hawkswold Sector.

"Fought on the Lorastir side," Coburn replied evenly. "I was twenty-one when the revolution overthrew the old monarchy."

Which would make her about fifty-eight now. Auntie Maru's age.

"You were a Republican?" Tessa asked as Fin watched.

His entire culture had sat out the war, other than selling anything to anyone with cash.

"Was," Coburn nodded. "Later, when Sigra made himself emperor, I became an Imperial. Was in the army for twenty-five years, then worked for the government for another few until they largely demobilized after *Vinoris*."

"And since then?" Tessa pressed, noting how the woman book-ended things well without filling in any details.

"Kicking around," Coburn shrugged. "I'd like for all the wars to be over. I have a nice enough pension that I don't have to work these days. It goes a lot further out on the Periphery than it does in the Arles Region. Plus, I wanted to see the sights."

Tessa gestured to the restaurant, accidentally making eye contact with the owner who had just emerged from the back. That man's eyes got huge for a moment and he looked around for Wyatt.

Tessa shook her head at the man and he seemed to relax.

"Trouble?" Coburn asked in a sharp, quiet voice.

"One of my crew got into a fight here a while ago," Tessa replied. "He's not allowed back in. As I was saying, how do the sights stack up?"

"A lot of the worlds out here are the same," Coburn nodded. "Raw and untamed. Filled with people struggling to get by, but free to do whatever they want. That's both a plus and a minus. The core worlds are a little too boring for me these days."

"Headed anywhere in particular?" Tessa pressed. "We're a tramp, so we go where the jobs are, rather than staying on a circuit. If you had a particular destination in mind, we might and might not be your best fit."

Coburn nodded.

"Mostly, I'm just being out here," she said. "Spent too long in uniform and following orders. Did some things I am not proud of admitting, but I own them nonetheless. I did have a question for you, Captain."

Tessa nodded.

"Your ship is named *Last Stand*," Coburn continued. "Any particular reason for that?"

"I was at *Vinoris*," Tessa said in a hard, quiet voice. "On the losing side. One of the few survivors of the battle and the camps afterwards. *Last Stand* reminds me of that, good and bad."

"Still a rebel?" Coburn asked in a careful, light voice.

"I was never a rebel, Coburn," Tessa said. "At the end, they came through town and grabbed every warm body that they could. At gunpoint. Gave us a few weeks of training, then threw us into battle. At that point, they had more guns than shooters."

"I see," Coburn nodded. "I wasn't at *Vinoris*. By then, I

was generally working on *Baramunz*, where I didn't stand out as much."

"Were you a spy?" Fin asked in that innocent, curious voice he did that got answers without offending people. He was good at that.

Coburn had almost forgotten he was there, from the way her head snapped around.

Then she shrugged.

"I suppose you could say that," she finally said after a moment of contemplation. "Wasn't hunting down the rebels like your Captain here, but the folks stirring them up and funding them, as long as they never got their own hands dirty."

"And today?" Tessa asked, hand wanting to stray down to the revolver on her thigh.

"The war's over, Captain," Coburn said firmly. "Isn't it?"

"The war? Yes," Tessa nodded. "But the Periphery is a hard place. Often lawless once you get off the surface of a planet. Sometimes when you get out of sight of the city limits on some worlds."

"I assume anybody out here not wearing an Ergrove uniform is probably mixed up in things that the local law enforcers frown on, Captain," Coburn nodded and spoke quietly. "Likely them as well. It is also no longer my job to enforce such things. I'm an old, fat woman who never married, never had kids, don't have any family to call my own after this long."

"What are you about, then?" Tessa asked.

"I've seen evil done, Captain."

Coburn turned so deadly serious that Tessa felt a chill settle in her stomach at the words.

"Done evil," the woman continued remorselessly. "Hell, I've *been* evil. Out here, I have time to try to reconcile all that and find peace. Reinvent myself as someone entirely else. Isn't that why folks come to the Periphery?"

"Some of them," Tessa allowed. "Others are being chased. Most come looking to make their fortune, but they're the young ones, wild-eyed and full of dreams."

"You're young," Coburn challenged her ever so slightly.

"I stopped being young at Clethorpe, Coburn," Tessa growled back. "Plus, I'm *Vlikine*. The only reason Zaddinul never wiped us out was that Lorastir invaded and the army was busy elsewhere. They still circled back a few times to try. As did others. Not a lot of my people left in the galaxy."

"Not looking for trouble, Captain," Coburn backed off. "Just wanted to make sure you knew where I was coming from."

Tessa considered it. Considered the woman. If she was working with those mercenaries, Tessa couldn't suss out how that would work, and she was pretty good at that sort of thing normally.

"If you don't mind the randomness of our flight, or keeping your mouth shut about things you might see, cost is two yuan a week," Tessa said. "You'll eat out of the common pot with the rest of us, but nobody ever goes hungry. And you'll do your own laundry. There will be times I ask you to remain in your cabin, or not leave the ship during a stop, but you can guess what happens then, so I won't spell it out more than that. Don't want any trouble, and I will dump you wherever we are if you give me any reason to."

"Honest," Coburn nodded. "Accountable, which is more than I can say for some of the other ships I inquired about around here."

She held out her hand and Tessa took it after a moment.

Food arrived right then and that seemed to be a pretty good sign.

Hopefully, she wasn't making a mistake with this one.

Scene Ten

Tessa rose and stretched. The owner had watched her and Fin like a hawk, but not bothered to come over and speak while they ate. Left them alone now, too. She left an extra jiao, a tenth of a yuan, over her normal tip as a thank you and headed for the door.

"We're leaving either later tonight, or first thing in the morning," Tessa reminded Laney Coburn.

"I will head up and grab my trunk now," the woman said. "I should be ready to board in fifteen minutes."

Tessa nodded and they stepped out of the restaurant into the evening gloom.

And right into trouble.

Four of them, just like before. Same four, looking closer. Dressed in black. Not tactical gear or uniforms, but dark clothing.

Closest two had pistols out and pointed at her before Tessa realized that those moving shadows were people.

"Captain Sladek," the third one said abruptly. "We need to go aboard your ship."

Tessa was more angry than shocked. And that was

mostly aimed at Wyatt, who hadn't done anything to warn her about this ambush.

"What the hell do you want?" she growled at them.

They had her, Fin, and Laney boxed in against the side of the building, past the shatterproof windows on black cinder block walls. Just shy of the alley they'd stepped out of.

Where the fuck was that worthless killer she kept on staff?

"We're looking for fugitives, Captain," the man growled back. No voices raised yet. She could hear a singer on a guitar somewhere with the windows open above and behind her. "There's a huge bounty on their heads."

"Only passenger I'm carrying right now is this woman," Tessa replied. "She the one you want?"

"No, she's way too old," the man sneered.

Tessa waited for Laney to speak, but the woman merely bristled and scowled.

"So who are you after?" Tessa asked, drawing this out.

Might be a case of mistaken identity. She could hope. Armor under her shirt would stop most bullets at this range, since they only had combat semi-auto pistols with short barrels. Would ruin her shirt. And her humor.

"Nataliya and Presley Horowitz," the man in charge of the group said. "Flight from Lorastir justice. Assaulting Imperial authorities. Whole list of crimes. Rumor says the women are on *Alfann*. We aim to find them."

"Why the hell are you bothering me?" Tessa asked.

"You got a rep," the leader said. "Plus, you work for Raven occasional-like. Ergrove Governor had him and a bunch of others arrested to keep those two women from escaping."

"Well, you aren't coming aboard my ship without a

sworn-out warrant and a legitimate deputy," Tessa informed the man. "Anything else makes you pirates and I'll shoot you down like dogs."

"You don't understand, Captain," he sneered. "We're armed and you aren't. We're doing this my way."

Tessa was all set to skin Wyatt alive for leaving her hanging like this. Unless they'd managed to sneak up on him, in which case the raw embarrassment might have caused him to die of shame already.

She was about to retort something tart and ugly when Laney held up a finger and took a half-step forward.

"A reward, you say?" Laney asked in a completely different tone and cadence than she'd had over dinner. Firm. Eloquent. Aristocratic, even. "Lots of money for them?"

"That's right," the leader nodded. "Five talents for the younger one and fifteen for her sister."

Shit, that was a lot of money. A talent was a thousand yuan, and a yuan was a good day's wages in a place like Weinsefeld Docks. That kind of money would pay off her mortgage to Zaddinul Intersystem Insurance and still leave her with a nice retirement nest egg earning interest someplace like Inleah.

"Oh, well in that case…" Laney started to say.

Tessa made the mistake of watching the woman, instead of the gunmen. That was okay, because they'd screwed up, too.

Laney took another half step forward, both fists coming up like whips to hit the two gunmen in the faces like hammers. Normally, just a stinger. Nothing that took a man out of a fight.

Then Laney grabbed both heads and slammed them together like coconuts. Ripe ones.

Tessa had blinked, but she had her revolver out.

The leader had flinched even worse when Wyatt appeared out of the dark alley and crunched the fourth man in the neck with *Brunhilde*, sending him down.

Suddenly, it had turned into four on one the other direction. He didn't make the mistake of provoking her. That was smart. Hands went up instead.

"Where ya been, Wyatt?" she asked, never taking her eyes off the leader.

"Had to maneuver around them when they decided to slip into my hiding spot in the alley," he said. "Been in there with them for an hour, but they never noticed me. Waiting for the idiot here to start monologuing so I could get something useful out of them. We know enough to shoot them in self-defense yet?"

Tessa smiled at the last stranger still standing. Law ran thin on the docks. She was also a known quantity, and these four were outsiders that had probably been making a lot of folks nervous.

Self-defense had elastic margins on *Alfann*.

Wyatt was covering the three down. Fin and Laney disarmed them as Tessa walked right up to the leader and rested her barrel against his chest.

Nicer dressed than the others. Black slacks, black shirt, black blazer. Even a black tie. Felt like a boss of a group of goons.

"Pirates, buddy," she said. "I don't have your fugitives. But if I ever see you or your boys again, I'm just going to open fire into the crowd and assume self-defense. Wyatt might even go hunting you, rather than waiting around. Do we have an understanding?"

"We do," the man said carefully.

Fin slid up next to him as she watched and a hand went into the inner pocket of the jacket, coming out with a wallet and folded papers. Pistol came out of the other side.

"Oh, good, you aren't another dumbass Masterson Op," Fin announced in a louder voice than necessary. Masterson wasn't a friend of little people on the Docks. They worked for the money. "Then lots of folks around here might also feel the need to hunt you."

He dropped the man's wallet on the brick pavers. Kept the gun.

"Hmmm," Fin continued. "Nataliya Horowitz. Presley Horowitz. Yup, about like he said. Couple of really pretty women folk. Nobody I know."

Fin folded up the wanted posters and slipped them into his own jacket pocket.

"She's not kidding, you know," Fin said brightly at the man. "I married her, after all. You and yours would best be suited to running like hell at this point, because I plan to file an attempted piracy complaint with the sheriff in the morning. With descriptions. Don't care if you call yourselves bounty hunters. From where I see it, you're just common brigands robbing honest folks. Law might be a little sketchy around here, but they'll give us a better listen than they will you."

Fin nodded and walked past the fellow. Tessa rotated around him as she did the same, pistol unwavering. She nodded thanks to Laney, and that woman turned a left at a hard, fast walk, words unspoken.

Wyatt leaned in.

"Self-defense," he stage-whispered to the man, then backed away.

Last Stand was down a few blocks, but a shuttle flew overhead at this moment, headed that direction. It sounded like Abigail's, even, which would be fantastic timing on everyone's part.

Get Abigail home. Get Laney aboard. Get off this rock.

She planned on answering the next door chime with

her pistol in hand and Wyatt hiding somewhere in the cargo hold, in case some fool tried to rush her.

Then they could be off *Alfann* and on to the next step of this messed up adventure.

Fin broke into a jog. She joined him. Wyatt moved silently and kept up. They got through all the foot traffic and back to the ship quickly.

Somehow, Tessa wasn't surprised when there were two more folks standing just outside her cargo hatch waiting for her.

SCENE ELEVEN

Tessa slowed to a walk. She still had her revolver in one hand, but that wasn't as uncommon a sight on the Strip as one might think. Especially running. At night. Fin and Wyatt also cut short the mad dash, though *Brunhilde* had vanished inside Wyatt's jacket.

Wouldn't be that hard to draw it again, so Tessa wasn't worried.

Married couple, from the look of them. Male and female. Expensively attired. Big steamer trunk that they were currently seated on.

Wife was in an ankle-length dress with petticoats to give it body. Empire waist. Long sleeves. Gloves. Pretty hat with the brim folded up above her eyes. Longish hair down and loose.

Husband wore slacks and an overcoat belted at his waist. Blazer was visible underneath, as was a white shirt and ascot. Clean-shaven. Wire-rimmed glasses. Black homburg on his head.

They perked up when Tessa and her boys emerged from the crowd of pedestrians and approached the hatch.

"Captain Sladek?" the man asked hopefully, rising to face her.

"And you might be?" Tessa countered.

Didn't holster the revolver. Didn't point it at him, either. Didn't answer his question.

"Constanz McLaren, madam," he said with a quick nod that almost felt like an autonomous tic. Heels even came together as he did, like a Court fop. "At your service. My wife, Brianna. I spoke with a member of your crew earlier about booking passage. She said you were at dinner, but would return shortly."

"So you just camped and waited for us?" Tessa asked.

"I did not wish to retire and run the risk of missing you, madam," he said in a voice she could only describe as *chipper*. "Nor to wake up in the morning and find that you had already departed. I find that portions of Weinsefeld were far less serene and genteel than we had originally been led to believe, and while the city itself is lovely, my finances do not currently stretch to staying in some of the less exciting and friendlier locales. Thus, I had hoped that you might be amenable to transporting us elsewhere."

She'd come to rest at a comfortable distance. Wyatt was beside her facing back. Fin waited expectantly.

"You go ahead and prep," she told her husband. "I'll get these folks and Laney sorted out shortly."

He nodded, kissed her on the cheek, and slid around the McLarens, keying the hatch and disappearing.

"Lots of other ships making the circuit," Tessa said to the strangers.

"I've asked around the immediate vicinity and you have a high reputation for probity, Captain," Mr. McLaren replied, again nodding. "Some of the vessels in dock strike me as hardly more than pirates in sheep's clothing, if you will pardon my casting possibly-undeserved accusations."

"No, you'd be right with some of them," she said. "Where was it you intended to go to?"

"At present, my interests lie more in departing *Alfann* and some of the social issues endemic to this world," McLaren replied. "Past that, we are on something of a promenade to celebrate our wedding. An extended honeymoon, if you will. Destinations will come and go as we enjoy ourselves seeing the outer rim worlds."

Tessa looked closer at the man now. Short and slender. Had a look of Zaddinul about him, but the cosmopolitan folks who were at the top of the social pyramid, rather than the workers at the bottom with her. Those aristocrats that married at their own level across national and cultural boundaries, rather than relying on geography. Nobleman of some sort obviously. She'd be willing to bet a yuan unseen that he had soft hands.

She looked at the wife as well, then did a double take.

Utterly, freaking gorgeous woman. Fair skin. Long brown hair. Perfect symmetry to her face in a way that was almost unnatural. Bright blue eyes that were so uncommon around here, with escaped serfs and workers from Zaddinul so thick on the ground.

If her husband was a Zaddinul noble, either on the run or merely deposed from his estates by the arrival of Lorastir forces, the wife was pure Lorastir. Probably the capital at *Falorea* itself.

Functionally, the center of the universe these days: politically, culturally, or socially.

She glanced over at Wyatt. The man had taken one look at the McLarens and subsequently ignored them to watch her back. She didn't think the mercs would try their luck again this quickly, but tomorrow was a whole other day and they might be getting feisty and desperate by then.

She needed to be gone. Now.

Either she carried the McLarens with her or dumped their asses right here on her landing ramp and called it good.

One more paying customer had been useful. Abigail's money kept them in food by herself but wasn't enough to keep them flying. Thus jobs for folks like Raven.

Laney would keep them above water until she found someone to take that iridium off her hands.

Two more? Hell, that was getting ahead on the mortgage or starting to put money away against not flying someday.

She'd long ago decided that she didn't want kids, but hadn't made any permanent changes, her or Fin. Just care and chemicals. Having a youngster would severely cramp her style as a criminal.

She just couldn't see showing up to rob a bank with an infant on her hip.

"Anybody chasing you right now?" Tessa asked, just to see how they reacted.

Both went a little too cold. A little too still, even. Not exactly a tell, but something.

"I expect that the locals might have seen us in our finery and become covetous, Captain Sladek," Mr. McLaren replied after a pause almost too short to be noticeable. "We do not really belong in a place like this."

"That's for certain," Tessa agreed. "Looking for names."

"I have no names of folks who might be after us at present," he said with a tilt of his head.

Something was a little off, but not bad. Probably on the run from her parents or something equally tedious. God knew that Fin's family had largely ostracized him for marrying her. Probably afraid of dark-complected kids running around at future reunions or something.

"Passage runs three yuan a week for the two of you," Tessa said challengingly. "Food from the common pot of whatever we make. Cabin for the pair of you. Do your own laundry. There will be times I ask you to remain in your cabin so as to keep you from getting dirty when we're taking on cargo."

"I find that rate acceptable, Captain," he said. "May I be so bold as to inquire about your next destination and expected itinerary?"

"Next stop's *Newhall* from here," Tessa said. "Not sure much past that, as we're dead-heading right now to negotiate our next run."

"Well, in that case, perhaps it was fortuitous that we came along," McLaren smiled. "Our transport fee will help offset and defray your operational costs."

Tessa was getting a headache just parsing his diction, but kept a smile on her face. Well-educated. High-born. Presumably wealthy, right up until something had gone wrong.

They didn't look like a pair of grifters on the run from the law, but she'd seen teams like that before. In this case, they weren't working so hard on the cover of newlyweds. Not like con artists selling you a pig in a poke.

"Gear?" Tessa asked.

McLaren turned to indicate the steamer.

"One trunk, Captain," he said. "Plus a few bags I had placed out of sight while we waited. If we have a deal, I shall retrieve them imminently."

Tessa nodded, and kept the revolver ready in case he came back with a gun or something. Didn't look like trouble.

Not that kind of trouble, anyway. The wife remained perfectly still, quietly seated all prim and proper.

Mr. McLaren slipped to the edge of the ship and

reached a hand to draw out a black leather satchel and an old-fashioned carpet bag from where he'd hidden them in the shadows caused by her ramp light.

Good place to keep them, if someone came along and wanted to rob you. She supposed that the big steamer had nothing but clothing and sundries, and the two bags were the important bits.

As he returned, she smiled.

"All weapons of any sort will be stowed in the ship's locker if you were traveling with any," she said. The tone didn't sound like a threat nearly as much as the words themselves did.

McLaren simply nodded.

"We are at present unarmed," he explained. "That was one of the reasons I wished to escape *Alfann* as quickly as possible. This is not a world for folks like myself and my wife."

Tessa let that one go. It might be her kind of place, but that just sketched the enormous social and cultural distance separating the two of them. Perhaps better than anything else she might find if she went looking.

"My dear," he said to his wife, holding out a hand for her to grasp while rising.

Brianna McLaren was shorter than her husband by a slight amount. Merely average in height for a woman. Athletic, though. Muscles and grace in her sleeves and neck. Tessa was willing to bet she had dancer's legs under all that frilly cloth.

Effective disguise, but you couldn't do anything about how stunningly beautiful she was, short of going beyond the hijab that Tessa hadn't worn tonight and settling down for something that completely covered the face.

If they were being hunted, Tessa might make a few suggestions. She had a couple of disguises in the back of the closet that she might pull out for the woman, depending.

Nothing like walking into a bank in a burqa or even a full niqab. With guns underneath.

Constanz McLaren touched a button and the steamer popped up on wheels. He pulled a leash control and turned to her expectantly.

Tessa put away her concerns and nodded to the man, moving past them to the hatch and keying in the code that opened the wider door. Easier than trying to get that trunk through.

She stepped back and guided them clear as it came down, revolver still in hand and attack dog nearby sniffing the night sky as only Wyatt could do.

Nobody was sneaking up on Wyatt Nakada tonight.

It was tomorrow that had her worried.

Scene Twelve

Tessa was up on the bridge, having gotten the McLarens' gear settled and them in the cabin aft directly across from Wyatt. Laney Coburn could go next to him aft one, so if the newlyweds made honeymoon noises, Wyatt wouldn't have to hear it.

The walls were thick enough to block most sound, but occasionally, to hear Auntie talk, you found the right rhythm for a harmonic that echoed through the whole vessel. That or Tessa had hit a certain plateau a few times and left air vents open.

She was the captain. The others could deal with it.

Abigail came forward from the shuttle dock. Normally, that door was locked, but she had a key. Easier than making her walk up and down stairs constantly when she wanted to find Tessa, who was often up here with Fin.

"I understand from Fin and Maru that you've almost got a full house, Captain?" Abigail said as she stepped in.

Tessa rose and turned to the woman.

Up until yesterday, Tessa would have said that Abigail

was the most beautiful woman Tessa had ever seen. Not anymore. Brianna McLaren was a whole step beyond merely stunning.

Tiny, when McLaren was much taller. Abigail ran maybe one hundred and fifty-five centimeters. Fifty kilograms soaking wet. Brown hair like the McLaren woman, but far curlier. The same perfect skin. The same glacial blue eyes.

"Retired soldier woman from Lorastir and a pair of newlyweds who might have eloped, but I didn't ask too closely," Tessa said. "The soldier helped us with some trouble on the Strip earlier. She's the last to arrive, and then we're gone, so I'm happy you cut your evening short."

Abigail nodded.

"Tedious would be an insult to the gentleman in question," she said. "Perhaps the situation. They almost grow predictable, to the point that I could have had the last half hour or so of conversation alone in my cabin and hardly missed a word."

"Another one madly in love you with and hoping that his money and connections would impress you?" Fin grinned up at her.

Those two had almost as complicated and interesting a relationship as Fin and Wyatt. In both cases, more siblings than anything. It worked.

"Worse," Abigail's eyes got big and excited. "He thought he had a magic penis that would make me fall in love with him."

They all shared a laugh at that.

"Most men think that way," Tessa chuckled.

"She only married me for my money," Fin said with a perfectly straight face. For about a second before he grinned.

"Well, if you aren't that good in bed, maybe I need to steal her away from you," Abigail sassed.

"Only if I get to watch," Fin countered.

"Hush, you two," Tessa interrupted before they got going.

Worse than teenagers. Or maybe she was just unnaturally old. All the light-years she'd gone and things she'd done.

"So where's next?" Abigail asked, turning into a far too serious businesswoman for being all of twenty-four years old.

But as she'd said, she'd spent a decade in school learning her trade. Business was a large part of that, because even the most beautiful woman could only rely on her looks alone for another decade or so.

Or, as an old mentor had told Tessa long ago, "Eventually, you have to roll over and talk to him."

Talking was what made Players rich. Beauty drew the moths, but Intellect held them.

"*Newhall*," Tessa said. "Had a problem with our most recent job."

"I heard a little birdy tell me that the authorities had decided to crack down hard on *Alfann*'s underworld," Abigail nodded. "I assumed someone like Raven would be on the chopping block but wasn't in a position to get you a message."

"And you shouldn't have tried, Abigail," Tessa replied seriously. "If we get in trouble, you should always have an alibi of ignorance."

She started to speak but Tessa interrupted her.

"You're more important than we are," Tessa reminded her. "You have the ear of wealthy and powerful people, even out here. We're all rats off the Strip. Nobodies. Your actions have bigger consequences than ours."

Abigail subsided. Then grinned.

"Haven't been to *Newhall* yet," she offered brightly. "What should I expect?"

"*Alfann* exists to make *Newhall* seem less seedy," Fin spoke up. "Barely. Generally, those systems are the bottom two on my demographic charts for Hawkswold Sector. You ought to be in a good position, though, as the economic pyramid there is even sharper than *Alfann*'s. Less underworld depth, so more of the money flows into the blue-blood's hands."

"I see," Abigail said, turning scholarly and serious. "And how long will we be there?"

"Either ten minutes, or several days," Tessa said. "I have an underworld contact to reach out to. If I have success, I'd like to dump my illicit cargo quickly, then work on getting some other job to move us from the scene of that crime. If *Newhall* is facing the same sort of crackdown, we're gone quickly."

"Would you prefer if I went ahead and found some clients anyway?" Abigail asked. "You can either wait patiently, or swing back by and get me."

"Let's pretend like nothing is wrong with our world," Tessa decided. "You do your thing, and we'll work around that. I got the feeling that my new passengers aren't just set to hop off there. Might lose the newlyweds if we went to *Beaumonde*, but even that's below what they're used to."

"Oh?" Abigail perked right up at that.

"Arles Region money," Tessa said with a sober nod that Abigail returned. "She's utterly gorgeous. He strikes me as both noble and smart, which is a rare, dangerous combination."

"Why in the world would they come to Hawkswold?" Abigail asked.

"Dunno," Tessa shook her head. "But if you felt like possibly charming that out of them at some point, it would help my peace of mind."

"Absolutely, Captain," Abigail said, then broke into a grin. "I've only finally gotten you folks trained to fly me around like I like. Last thing I want to do is find a new ship and start over."

Tessa rolled her eyes at the woman, but understood. They'd had a few quiet conversations where Abigail suggested that she understood how much her own Lorastir background and money had come from conquering the rest of civilized space over the last generation.

She hadn't come right out and said that *Last Stand* was her way of saving someone, but it had been intimated.

Tessa was smarter than she was proud, and allowed it. Plus, having a Player as a long-term passenger meant that she could land just about anywhere and most Port Authorities would welcome her. Made smuggling a lot easier that way.

Hell, in some of the more backwards, out of the way places, they'd set Abigail up on a stage, or an auditorium if they could afford one, and let her just Play: telling stories, singing, and performing for folks able to kick a few jiao coins into a pot. County Fair kind of entertainment in places where they hardly got that.

They couldn't save everyone, but Tessa was happy that Abigail was willing to try.

The rear hatch chime sounded.

"That should be Laney," Tessa said. "Abigail, if you're docked and ready, we might be five minutes from departure."

"All set, Captain," the woman said. "You go aft. I'll settle in the dining hall and have some tea so I have a chance to meet your new guests in relaxed circumstances."

"Thank you," Tessa said. Then she turned and found the intercom switch.

"Wyatt, headed aft."

Scene Thirteen

Tessa had crossed the top deck to check in on Auntie Maru and update her, then came down the stairs in the cargo bay. Wyatt was already there, ducked behind a stack of boxes with *Doomripper* in hand and ready for mayhem.

She always felt much better about answering the main door when fools trying to hijack her would get shot dead for their troubles. One of the reasons she kept a fellow like Wyatt around.

He stayed with the crew because she was willing to be in charge and all he generally had to do was follow orders. Some men were like that.

She left the rifle in the box and touched the revolver on her hip once, mostly as a security blanket. Fin was ready to fly. Maru was tending her engines. Abigail would play hostess.

Tessa just had to get one last thing done, then head to *Newhall* and hopefully find a buyer for a lot of stolen iridium. She checked the rear camera. Nobody visible in the fisheye beyond Laney, standing there with a much smaller trunk than the McLarens and what looked like saddle bags for a horse slung over her shoulder.

Weird, but not that weird, she supposed. Some of these worlds had more horses than motor vehicles. Easier to maintain, since two horses could make more, while your tractor would eventually break down.

Tessa opened the hatch and smiled at the older woman. Only the gray hair really gave away her age, as she didn't have flabby skin or liver spots on her hands. Crow's feet around the eyes and mouth, but that could be anything after forty, depending on the woman.

"Am I on time?" Laney asked as she stepped to the hatchway.

"Barely," Tessa grinned. "We picked up a pair of other passengers at the last minute, and have been waiting for you."

"Related to our friends out on the street?" Laney asked cautiously.

"I doubt it," Tessa said. "Young newlyweds on a honeymoon promenade. Got them settled and we're launching as soon as you're ready."

"All I have is this," the older woman said. "Where should it go?"

"The trunk can stay out here for now, or you can roll it into your cabin," Tessa said. "Might be a tight fit, since the rooms are compact."

"I'll leave it here," Laney decided. "I can travel anywhere for a week out of my saddlebags anyway."

"This way, then," Tessa said, hitting the button to close the hatch and lock it. She brought the comm live. "Fin, we're closed up here. You can leave now as long as you don't fly crazy."

"Would I do that?" he asked back. "No wait. Don't answer that."

Tessa chuckled. Laney raised an eyebrow.

"He's the best pilot I know, hands down," Tessa said. "And occasionally, he has to prove it."

"Understood," Laney said.

They walked to a spot near where the McLaren trunk was. Wyatt stood up from behind it and slung *Doomripper* over his shoulder. Between them, they opened a spot for Laney's case and got it in.

"Wyatt, the rifle can go away for now," she informed him.

He looked at her for a long moment, then nodded. She watched him move to the arms locker and enter the access code. *Doomripper* went in and he closed it.

Tessa assumed *Brunhilde* was still hidden away somewhere. Not that she didn't trust her new passengers, but prepared is prepared.

"I'm for a nap," the big man announced. "Or maybe just bed."

"I'll see you in the morning," she replied.

He moved quickly and she let him get a head start. Laney was looking around the cargo bay with an appraising eye.

"Randovall Nucleonautics Light Tumbrel?" she asked.

Tessa nodded, a bit surprised. They were old, and had never been common.

"Flew aboard one for a few years," Laney said, nodding. "You'd have about been in diapers then."

Tessa nodded back. That had been more than a decade after the Lorastir Revolution that threw down the old Monarchy. Revolutionary General Amarns Sigra had later brought it all back, crowning himself Emperor. And conquering most of the civilized parts of the galaxy along the way.

Ergrove was strong enough to remain independent.

Inleah was neutral and largely amoral, so they served their own purpose. Other nations beyond that scope weren't any sort of threat nowadays, save that they might be targets of some future military adventure.

One of these days, Tessa supposed she'd need to know more about Laney Coburn's past, but it could wait. Or she could sic Abigail on the woman and let her charm it out.

Laney was looking at her expectantly. Like she knew what questions were coming. Tessa surprised the woman by turning and heading up the corridor after Wyatt instead.

"This is the cargo deck," Tessa gestured as she walked. "Two shuttles directly overhead, with the engines between them and the engine room forward from there and the bridge all the way at the bow. Those are off limits unless you are accompanied, but you shouldn't have any reason to be on the top deck anyway, unless coming up to talk to me or Fin."

Laney had stretched her legs from the surprise and caught up.

"Four cabins aft," Tessa continued as they exited the cargo bay. "You'll be in L3 for now. R3 is empty. Wyatt is in L2 next to you and the McLarens are in R2 across from him. If you want to drop your bag here, I can give you the nickel tour."

She keyed the hatch and stepped aside for Laney.

Inside, the room was sparse. Three and a half meters deep, give or take the way the outer hull curved and cable runs and ducts intruded. Queen-sized day bed in one corner with space underneath where Laney could eventually stow her trunk with a little work. Armoire bolted down in the other corner, with a chair for reading.

Laney set her saddle bags on the bed and nodded. No art on the walls, but that was laziness on Tessa's part. She rarely had customers who could afford the cabins. Usually, they'd get stuffed into one of the coffins.

"This way," Tessa said, moving forward again. "Coffin rooms for broke travelers. Three-by-three on each side, currently all empty. A meter-two wide and tall, and twice that deep. Cozy for one. Cramped if you had two. Folks have done it."

"I like space to stretch my arms," Laney said dryly.

"Agreed," Tessa nodded. "This is the linen closet and laundry room. Across is the general bathroom, which you will be sharing with everyone. The forward two cabins where Fin, I, and Auntie Marusya bunk have en-suite, so we're not competing with you for anything but hot water. Showers will run for five minutes, then they are programmed to wait fifteen before starting again, so you'll want to be quick."

"The army usually set them to three minutes, so five will be a luxury," Laney laughed.

Yes, she supposed it would be.

"Forward, this is the dining hall with kitchenette," Tessa said as they entered. "As you can see, we grow a lot of spices and things, both hydroponically and in pots, that frequently go into dinner. Please don't touch anything without permission, as they can be a bit fragile."

"That's oregano, and that one's mint, Captain," Laney replied. "Fragile is not the term that immediately comes to mind for those two."

"No, but the peppers and tomatoes are," Tessa laughed. At least the woman knew her plants. "We'll generally eat here, and this is open for passengers at all hours. Tea and coffee are in the pantry next to the stove."

"I also packed some tea, so I might just add it to your larder," Laney said.

"That would be helpful," Tessa acknowledged. "We try

to keep a broad selection, but it can be a crapshoot. Finally, this is the commons. Rec room. As with the dining hall, more plants. Entertainment suite is here with some videos. We have a pretty good selection of book reels, but only one Personal Analytical Engine."

"I brought my own," Laney said. "As well as a variety of books myself. It will be interesting to see what your library looks like."

"Random," Tessa grinned. "Pawn shops. Estate sales. Occasionally things that a previous passenger forgot when they departed."

"Will there be pawn shops or bookstores at our next stop, Captain?" Laney asked.

Tessa shrugged.

"I'm sure there are," she said. "Not the sort of places I spend a lot of time in."

"I see," Laney nodded. "Perhaps I will need to see what I can find to improve your library, then."

"That's unnecessary," Tessa countered.

"I find well-read folks to be the most interesting, Captain," Laney turned serious.

"Then you and Abigail will get along well," Tessa said, as the Player entered from forward, a mug of tea steaming in one hand.

"Abigail Blackford, meet Laney Coburn," Tessa introduced them. "Laney, Abigail is a certified Player who travels with us and rents one of the shuttles up top, but frequently dines with the crew. Abigail, Laney is a retired soldier and bureaucrat from Lorastir."

"Charmed," Abigail smiled up at the so-much-larger woman.

"Similarly," Laney bowed over the hand they shook. "I was just talking to the captain about books and perhaps the need to expand the library here."

"That would be excellent," Abigail replied. "I despair of things occasionally, but I do what I can."

Tessa rolled her eyes at the performance those two were putting on.

"If you will pardon me, I need to see how my husband is doing," she said, backing away and departing.

Last Stand was already in the air. Hopefully, nobody was trying to follow them, though they'd be hard-pressed to keep up, once Fin noticed them.

She needed to get to *Newhall* and try her luck.

Hopefully, it was turning for the better.

Scene Fourteen

Tessa was on the bridge with a mug of coffee in one hand when she heard footfalls climbing up. Wasn't Fin or Wyatt, as they both moved silently. She turned to see Abigail come into view.

The last two days had been quiet, getting out of *Alfann* and most of the way to *Newhall*. Probably a half day faster than anybody else could have done it, but Fin was exceptional when it came to flying. And other things.

Abigail moved to the co-pilot seat. Fin would be along soon, but he'd slept in a little this morning, happy for the last of the oatmeal and some sweet rolls that Maru had saved for him.

"How are the passengers doing?" Tessa asked.

Abigail had been utterly charming, as only she could do. That had gone a long ways towards making everything run smoother. Useful, when three strangers dropped in on five old friends. Well, good enough friends. Folks Tessa had accumulated over the last five years, how about that?

"Quite interesting," Abigail replied. "Laney is both far

more and far less than she appears at first glance. I haven't dug too deep, but have started mapping things in my own mind."

"And the McLarens?" Tessa asked.

"There are certain questions I would like to ask, but have refrained so far," Abigail said, her lips pursed and her brow furrowed.

"Such as?" Tessa asked, glancing at the stairs. Someone might stand at the bottom and listen, unless she shut the hatch right now. Didn't feel necessary, though she reserved the right to change her mind.

"Constanz presents as male," Abigail said quietly, as though also sensing the need for secrecy. "However, I am reasonably confident that he is a she. Or perhaps used to be, though I'm not sure that anybody without my level of training in people and presentation would have realized it."

"Does it matter?" Tessa asked. "His identcard shows male."

"He has a woman's hips," Abigail said quietly. "And jaw. Feminine structure that a man generally doesn't get."

"So?"

Abigail shrugged.

"Ergrove is far more concerned about that sort of thing than Lorastir," she said.

"Zaddinul was also wound a little too tight on the question," Tessa replied. "But this is the Periphery. Though I suppose that would explain why they had to leave the Arles Region. Forbidden love and all that. Things for poets and bards to get worked up about. Luckily, I have an expert on the topic handy."

"Funny," Abigail replied, throwing in her own eye roll and a grin. "But you don't mind?"

"I managed to get Fin largely disowned," Tessa reminded the woman. "But he seems to be happy."

"Probably," Fin said as he popped up onto the deck. "What did I do this time?"

"Married me," Tessa said.

"Single smartest thing I have ever done," he nodded. "Even a pilot's license is a distance second, and you know how much I love to fly."

He stepped close and kissed her. Smartest thing she'd ever done, too.

"Anything I need to worry about before I start plotting the last jump into *Newhall*?" he asked, looking brightly at the two women.

"Not at all," Tessa said, rising.

Outside the windows, Flightspace was its usual endless darkness where gravity wells of stars and nebulae showed as shades of color, from the deep indigo of a small planet all the way up to a white hot supermassive black hole.

"Good," he said. "Assuming I guessed right on the last jump, we should be on the ground in Astoria right about dinner time. If not, we'll come in around midnight and be there for breakfast. We know what to expect?"

She glanced at Abigail, but the woman knew most of their secrets. And still liked them.

"We need a new broker," Tessa said. "Or several. Hoping that Bao Li will do, and that she has fond memories of me, if she even remembers me at all."

"Any risk of bad things?" Abigail asked.

"It's been a few years," Tessa said. "Lots can change. Especially if Ergrove is finally thinking about cleaning up the Hawkswold Sector."

Fin laughed at that, but she knew that things would flow outwards from Weinsefeld Docks, carrying word and old rivalries with them, especially if a whole cast of tramp shippers like her were suddenly left in the lurch.

Three passengers helped.

Tessa just hoped that none of their secrets would cause a blowback with her and hers.

SCENE FIFTEEN

TESSA LOOKED AROUND THE ASTORIA WHARF WITH A discerning eye, seeking the flavor of the changes that might have arrived from *Alfann*. Astoria wasn't as bad as Weinsefeld, but that also wasn't a particularly high bar to clear, when you got right down to it.

Wharf Row was longer and ran with two sides inside the berm and fence that mostly provided a psychological barrier to the city outside. Anybody could climb over it or slip under easy enough. And it wasn't like the port authorities cared all that much, as long as you paid a fee on landing and then every week you were on the ground.

The sun was setting overhead at this moment. Late spring here, just verging over to summer heat soon. The rains ought to still run another few weeks, but they'd landed to clear skies and dry ground.

She turned to Fin and Maru.

"Abigail is already making calls, so I expect her to possibly depart, though not until tomorrow," she reminded them. "Wyatt and I will go talk to Bao Li and see what she might have available for us."

"The passengers all know that we might only be on the ground for a few hours," Fin nodded. "They are staying put for now, though I expect them to possibly go shopping ashore tomorrow, depending."

"Hopefully, it will be safe for them," Tessa said, glancing back and making sure that the cargo bay was currently empty.

Folks were in their cabins presently, after dinner. Too early to go to sleep, but there had been a taste in the air of quiet time.

All the better, since she didn't need grief from them on top of everything she might be bringing on herself.

"Lock us out," Tessa said. "I'll comm when we get back."

"Will do," Fin said, slipping close for a quick hug and kiss.

Tessa headed out into the gathering gloom. She and Wyatt had pistols on hips, but she expected the same from at least a quarter of the folks she'd see. Not as high a number as Weinsefeld Dock, but again, not much lower.

Because the Wharf ran long and curved, inside the port, there wasn't nearly as much foot traffic on the main road. More electric carts hauling trailers or flatbedding stuff around, so you had to stay to the side of the right of way most of the time. Or get honked at and maybe run over if someone wasn't paying attention.

Or some drunk had stolen a cart and was joyriding.

They walked. Sailors coming and going surrounded them, either headed into town for a drink, or heading back to relieve someone else for their turn. Largely civilized-looking folk. Wyatt still stayed close.

Outside the main gate, it smelled more like a street party. Like maybe she'd lost track of the local calendar and *Mardi Gras* or *Holi* was going on.

Tessa had too much armor under her shirt to get herself any beads, even if she cared that much. More than a few folks propositioned one or both of them as they walked.

She could see Wyatt slipping off to have a little local fun, but the job always came first with him. Especially if she had to blast out of here in a hurry because someone had posted a warrant for *All Known Associates* on Raven and a few others.

Tessa didn't really know Astoria City all that well, though the fish'n'chips shop operating out of a dead courier on the edge of the port had been there forever. She walked past it, considering the need for grease and potatoes later.

Instead, she strode down to a walk-up bar that sold drinks in paper cups to go. Small servings and crushable cups meant that it wasn't where you went when looking for a fight. There was a reason it was called *Wet Your Whistle*.

Enrique offered no outdoor seating anywhere nearby. You walked up, paid, drank, left.

She did now.

"Something easy," she said when Enrique recognized her. She put a jiao coin down on the counter.

Didn't matter what you ordered. You were getting pure alcohol that had been cut with water. From there, food coloring and maybe a little sugar and syrup to flavor it.

Sure wasn't rum made from cane or beets.

"Here you go, Captain," he said, handing her a cup full of blue. "Something for the big man?"

"Gonna get real booze, Enrique?" Wyatt grinned down at the man.

"This is real, Wyatt," Enrique said, only mildly put out.

"So's slash distilled from a coolant system," Wyatt replied. "Which is most of what you sell."

Enrique chuckled.

"So what can I do for you, Captain?" he asked, looking back over her shoulder.

Most of the folks, like Wyatt, were headed into town to drink at real bars, though there wasn't any rain right now.

Enrique made as much money from watching folks come and go as he did selling them alcohol.

"Trouble on *Alfann*," she said. "Felt like time to pick up stakes and explore other opportunities for a while."

"Oh?" he asked. "Worse than Raven being arrested?"

She ended up giving him a highly expurgated version of the story about the mercenaries and some of the other shenanigans on Weinsefeld Dock, over and above the crackdown.

Enrique nodded sagely.

"Nothing like that happening around here," he said. "At least not yet. Looking for a new dealer?"

"Contact back there suggested Bao Li," Tessa replied quietly, also glancing around. Wyatt was watching things like a hawk. "She still around?"

"She is," Enrique nodded.

He gave Tessa an address in one of the nicer parts of town. Not too nice. It was still Astoria. Nice enough that she was glad she'd showered and put on a better shirt today.

Tessa nodded and headed uptown, Wyatt in tow.

The place turned out to be a restaurant, but one of those joints that advertised as a private club, with two beefy bouncers at the door *checking reservations* and turning away folks. Mostly tourists who had wandered up the wrong sidewalk.

Tessa didn't know either man, and they got a lot of attention when she and Wyatt walked up, both armed. One of the two signaled inside and she was confident that more bouncers were coming. Armed ones, this time.

She stopped a respectable distance away and nodded to the smarter-looking one.

"Tessa Sladek," she introduced herself. "Hoping to have a word with Bao Li if she's available. I don't have a reservation."

He pulled out a clipboard anyway and looked, then wrote her name down.

"Nature of your business?" he asked in a voice that almost sounded friendly.

Almost.

"Business," she smiled. "Just in from *Alfann* and have some cargo I was hoping I might be able to sell into the local market."

"You're armed," he noted, as if just seeing the holster on her thigh for the first time.

"It's Astoria," she countered. As if that covered it all.

Might. It *was* Astoria.

"You wait here," he instructed.

As the man moved inside the door, two others appeared. Just as big as the one remaining. Looked like stun wands in their hands, which was a bit uncalled for.

Still, beggars and choosers. She stepped to the side and waited, watching inwards because Wyatt appeared to be ignoring the three at the door to watch the sidewalk behind her.

Appeared to be ignoring them. If one of them made a sudden move, she had no doubt how that man would react. He was bigger than any of them. Meaner, too. Those three were just jumped-up pretty boys in matching, off-the-rack suits that didn't fit.

The first bouncer returned a few minutes later.

"She'll see you," he said. "Your friend can wait outside. With your gun."

Tessa nodded and started unhooking everything before handing it to Wyatt. He put it around his waist backwards, with her gun on his left. Awkward way to draw.

She figured he'd find a way if it became necessary.

Still, Tessa found it funny that she got escorted in by three bouncers. Her unarmed and weighing half what any one of them did. She didn't think she had that bad a rep. Or that Bao Li would have that bad a memory of her.

If so, Wyatt might be earning his keep today.

The woman was seated in a back, corner booth. The restaurant was otherwise empty, save employees. Maybe it was a little early for entertainment, but the joint looked more like a private supper club that existed solely to launder money. She'd known a few in her time. It was a great gig if you could afford to pay off the tax authorities to look the other way.

Bao Li sat facing out. She was short and a little rotund. What Laney might have been, smaller and not exercising as religiously as that one had aboard *Last Stand*.

This woman looked about forty, and had come from the Chen Sector originally. Way the hell out beyond Zaddinul somewhere, where Zaddinul had generally faced towards Lorastir and Altenfeld as the more civilized folk. Almost the Periphery, where Ergrove was a constant menace.

They were like that.

Wide, almond-shaped eyes. Black hair that should have had more gray, considering the woman's age. It was cut in a short buzz, so she must have gotten it colored recently if so.

Or maybe it wasn't going to turn colors yet.

"Sladek," Li said as Tessa stopped a few meters away, pointedly not invited to sit. "Been a while."

Tessa nodded politely.

"Four years," Tessa offered.

"Grison still pissed at you?" Li asked with a hard grin.

"Hard to say," Tessa shrugged. "Probably more pissed that his new pilot and I ran off and got married. Haven't seen *Will-o-Wisp* or Mase Grison in a couple of years."

"He got picked up after you left," Li laughed like a tin bowl full of brass parts being shaken rudely. "Girl he hired to replace that pilot wasn't as good."

"Nobody's as good as Fin," Tessa said.

"I'd heard you married the boy," Li nodded. "Bought yourself a ship. Gonna settle down and make babies?"

"Shit, no," Tessa scowled. "Not the lifestyle for that. I'd have to go back to the Arles Region if I wanted to do something that silly."

"So what brings you to *Newhall*, Captain Sladek?" Li pivoted into a sharp, businesswoman's tone.

Tessa automatically glanced around, but the room was empty. Bouncers on three points of a triangle around her. Waiter and waitress over keeping the bartender babe company.

Nobody else.

"Everybody here works for me," Li said unnecessarily.

"I was working for Raven before," Tessa said.

"Heard that," Li grinned. "Heard he's got trouble these days."

"If so, nothing he didn't bring down on himself," Tessa nodded. "Man can be a handful."

The woman roared with laughter at that.

"Sit," she commanded, once she got control.

Tessa slid into the booth across from the woman. All

three bouncers continued to hover. Bao Li gestured to the bar.

"Get you something?" she asked.

"A rum sour blended wouldn't go to waste," Tessa replied.

"Not straight?"

"Woman's got to keep her head about her when dealing with a business shark like yourself," Tessa grinned.

That got a nod of approval.

Finding a new broker was like finding a new spouse. Dating fraught with difficulty.

Worse, Bao Li was far more than Raven. He was merely a fence at the end of the day. Bao Li was also a fixer. If you had a problem with the local authorities, she *fixed* it for you. Fence. Dealer. Recruiter.

High-powered badass in a gray tunic that looked like it had been washed down from black a few years ago. Comfortable and broken in.

"So what brings you to my door, hat in hand, Sladek?" Li asked as a glass got put down.

"Raven had me on a job when he was still a free man," Tessa replied. "My end was successful, but obviously, I ain't getting paid for it at this point. So I'm out some money and some time, and got a few things stashed away that I'd rather not be carrying around. Hoping to find someone who had a cousin that might be in need."

"Where did Raven send you?" Li asked.

"*Orvan*," Tessa said simply.

The woman's eyebrows rose.

"Interesting," she said. "Story was that a Masterson Op fought off a raid by a small army of killers in protecting that cargo."

Tessa laughed.

"One man, unarmed save a flashlight," she replied.

"Walked in without checking and raised a ruckus. My associate on your front sidewalk whomped him on the head when he wasn't looking. We handcuffed him to a box while we made our getaway. Took a box that Raven had been terrible interested in. Nobody died while I was around. If Masterson can't hire better and more honest folk, I'm not one to correct them."

"Nobody mentioned boxes disappearing," Li noted dryly.

Tessa shrugged and sipped. Excellent rum. Just the right amount of sweet and sour underneath it, plus crushed ice. Bao Li ran a top-shelf organization.

"Who suggested you come here?" Bao Li asked, turning the conversation.

"Dewey at Three Rocks," Tessa said.

"Old Dewey did that?" Li asked, intrigued.

Tessa nodded.

"He must like you, kid."

"Always done right by me," Tessa offered. "Tried to do right by him. You can never have too many friends in this business."

"Ain't that the truth?" Li replied.

She appeared to be relaxing, but Tessa wasn't about to let her guard down.

"And what did Raven send you after?"

"Twenty-four small bars of Tool-grade iridium," Tessa said quietly.

Bao Li whistled.

"That's over thirty kilograms," the woman noted. "And you got away with it?"

Tessa nodded.

"Must have been an inside job, to know that was there," Li said. "And the Masterson Op wasn't hurt, save for his dignity?"

"Had no reason to kill the fellow, after we disabled him," Tessa said.

"Not everyone would make that calculation," Li countered. "He could identify you later."

"And him dead would have likely caused Masterson bosses to hire somebody big and competent to come gunning for me as revenge," Tessa said. "I prefer flying below the level of scanners. Easier to make a living if you don't have the big players mad at you."

"Interesting logic," Li noted.

"Galaxy works better if we aren't killing each other all the time," Tessa replied.

Li nodded.

"So what was Raven offering to pay you?" Li asked.

Tessa knew a trap when she heard one. Bao Li probably already knew those numbers, so this was a way to judge someone's honesty.

Tessa told her the exact number, with a caveat.

"My assumption was that he already had a buyer in place," Tessa said. "So he'd recoup his expenses quickly. I appreciate that you might not. That you might need some time to arrange something. I'm fine working this for a discount, because I'd rather they be off my deck entirely in the short term."

"Lot of folks would want to dicker hard and whine about this point," Li noted sharply.

"How many of them will still be in the business in five years?" Tessa asked. "Or will they have been driven out, thrown in jail, or just given up and gone straight?"

"What will Raven say if he gets out of jail?" Li asked back.

"Is that likely?" Tessa countered. "Or is he going to be spending a lot of time breaking rocks on a penal asteroid?"

"The stories I've heard are of two minds," Li nodded.

"Well, him being in jail kind of cramps my ability to do business with him," Tessa smiled. "If he'd been willing to offer me a percentage up front, I might have been more willing to hold onto his cargo. As it is, I took all the risk and got left holding the entire bag, so I'm not feeling entirely benevolent on the situation."

"Understood, Captain," Li said. "You be around for a bit?"

"Unless you don't think you can deal," Tessa answered. "In that case, I'd be off to find someone else to work with. If you're of an open mind, I can hang tight for a few days while gears work."

"Excellent, Captain Sladek," Li nodded. "I'll ask around and be in touch."

Tessa emptied her glass and slid out of the booth, recognizing that for the dismissal it was.

"Thank you, ma'am," she said as her escorts formed up around her.

She got to the front door and nodded to Wyatt. He fell in silently as he handed her back her holster. Armed, they made their way into the darkness of Astoria's night.

"Anybody likely to be coming after us?" he asked a few blocks later in a tone she could only classify as hopeful.

"Won't know for a few days," Tessa said. "She'll make some inquiries with some other folks. Passengers are welcome to wander around town while we wait."

He fell silent and they made their way back to *Last Stand*.

At least the mercenaries weren't around to bother them.

SCENE SIXTEEN

Laney didn't like to admit to jealousy, but she was old enough to recognize that feeling for what it was. She'd never been all that attractive, even on her best days forty years ago. Solid. Muscular bulk, instead of athletic grace.

Brianna McLaren was simply the most beautiful woman Laney had ever met. Anywhere. Even more so than Abigail Blackford, though she didn't have nearly the education and experience to carry a conversation. But that was the whole point of being a Player.

So Laney kept her thoughts to herself and enjoyed the McLarens as slightly-shallow, well-bred fops. Immaculately dressed at all times, if a bit prissy and effete in the case of Constanz.

Today, Laney was at the hatch of *Last Stand*, preparing to go out and ransack the local pawnshops and arcades of Astoria for more interesting books to read. She had a dozen of her favorites on rolls for her reader, but once you could start quoting long sections of a book from memory, it was time to move on.

The McLarens were nearby, preparing to depart as

well. She even had a parasol this morning. That seemed to be the perfect accessory to her dress. It even matched Constanz's ascot.

Captain Sladek had confirmed last night that they would be around for a few days, so Laney had unpacked all her vests and hung them in the armoire. She had exactly two pairs of straight-legged trousers in slate gray wool. A half-dozen folded collar shirts that she always wore open-necked. All white.

More than half her trunk was vests, a vast, stylish selection that ran the rainbow of colors and textures. She'd spent too many years—decades really—dressed to vanish in any company. It was nice to be able to stand out. Today was a crimson paisley day.

Plus her mostly-empty saddlebags slung over one shoulder.

"Are you by chance headed into town?" Constanz asked as he and his wife stepped close, her hanging on his elbow.

"Shopping more than sightseeing," Laney nodded. "A few sundries for myself. Perhaps some more exotic teas. I'm primarily on the lookout for new book spools to read."

"Are you familiar with Astoria?" he asked.

"No," Laney replied. "But most such cities fall along a particular spectrum."

She studied the man's face. And the woman's beauty.

"Was there anything I might find for you while I'm out?" she asked, noting the hesitancy. "Or perhaps direct you as to where the seeking might be more fruitful?"

Nice folks. Well-educated, but in that useless sort of liberal arts quantity that let you have interesting conversations about esoteric topics, without the experience of ever getting one's hands dirty.

Laney had extensive experience with dirty hands, so to speak.

"We are unfamiliar with the city," Constanz replied in clipped, measured tones. "And with many such places, as we are fresh from the Arles Region and perhaps underprepared for life on the Periphery. Would you be offended if perhaps we were to travel into town with you today while we established our bearings?"

A lifetime of army and then…*other*…government work allowed Laney to translate that into something understandable. Folks didn't want to get mugged in town.

And it would let Laney spend more time drifting into the background, crimson paisley notwithstanding. She still wasn't used to not having to vanish at the drop of a hat or the discharge of a firearm.

"As long as I don't bore you, Mr. McLaren," Laney nodded.

"Please, call me Constanz," he countered. "We have spent several days aboard this ship, and neither appears to be ready to depart at *Newhall*. We should be on friendly, personal levels."

"Constanz," Laney nodded.

"And I," Brianna spoke up.

She was the quiet one, hardly ever speaking and seemingly relying on her husband for many things. There had been times when Laney had wondered if the woman was entirely right in the head, but that wasn't the sort of thing you asked strangers over dinner.

"Brianna," Laney said. "My pleasure. Shall we?"

She turned and they followed her to the hatch and outside. Morning in Astoria promised to be glorious, with a clear sky and the temperature already pleasant. A breeze and the afternoon would be perfect. Laney considered borrowing a camp chair from the Captain, merely so she could find a south facing and soak up some sun later.

It had been nearly forever since she'd had that kind of independent freedom.

"Was there something in particular you thought to seek?" Laney asked as they traversed the long stretch into town, occasionally bumping sailors and others going places in more of a hurry.

"Air and sunshine," Brianna spoke up, mildly surprising Laney. "I've spent too much time cooped up and needed this."

That much was obvious, as the woman was relaxing with every step taken. Constanz seemed preternaturally alert, but he was a small man in a galaxy that didn't always impart law and order. People like Wyatt Nakada had an unfair advantage.

Not around Laney, but he had also been more of a gentleman than she'd been expecting for the sloppy way he dressed and spoke.

Nakada still moved like a killer. She recognized that in the man.

Laney considered the economic architecture of a place like Astoria. She'd never been here, but they all followed certain rules of urban geography, regardless of the planet. Places generating the most profit from preying on sailors and ships would be closest to the main gate. Bars and temples of prostitution.

She didn't feel the need for touch. Male or female, though she supposed that Abigail Blackford might be an exceptional companion if and when she did. Young, brilliant, driven, artistic, and broadly educated.

Exactly what a Player was supposed to be.

"My thought is to move towards the far end of the strip outside," Laney said, thinking aloud for her companions.

"I'll know when we get outside the wire which direction to pick. From there, walk a certain proportion of the overall, stop, and work my way back. Is that amenable?"

"Why only a certain proportion?" Constanz asked, curious.

"Shops will rise in density, then quickly fall off past a certain point," Laney said. "To be replaced by food stalls, basic bodegas, and housing in declining quality and expense. I'm not going that far today."

Brianna nodded, almost unconsciously, as if she'd had the same logic, though Laney couldn't tell what the woman might have seen or done in her time to know such things. Or was that why she occasionally seemed damaged? Something bad had happened in such a place?

Not Laney's issue to deal with. But if sailors came along and felt the need to be a problem, Laney understood that she had also assumed unto herself the role of bodyguard today.

At least she had much practice.

It helped that Constanz kept up a genial conversation, mostly questions about geography and architecture. Some things went beyond Laney, but she did have a better appreciation of how smart the fellow was, to know some of those things.

At one point, when the crowds around them had thinned, Laney grew bold.

"Constanz, what was it you did before traveling to the Periphery?" she asked in an off-hand tone that didn't sound like an interrogation.

Good Cop, as it were.

"I was a medical doctor," he said. "A surgeon. I suppose that I still am, but obviously haven't been working of late. Traveling instead."

Laney nodded and dropped the topic as if she had

nothing more than idle curiosity. That did explain many things, though. A man who mostly worked with his mind, doing only delicate things with his hands. Yes, that fit Constanz McLaren nicely.

"I think this should be our point of reversal," Laney said as she measured the shops around her. The smells of grease and soup were growing stronger, suggesting food courts and trucks from here.

"I am happy to follow where you lead, Laney," Constanz nodded.

Laney let that one go and turned towards a shop half-hidden behind a brick arcade made up of several dozen arches holding up a porch. They suggested either intense summer heat or deluges of rain that should be fended off, but she didn't know *Newhall* enough to guess which. Perhaps both.

The shop was a bit of everything, which was Laney's intent. Not a pawn shop, exactly, but the place that might be an old-fashioned local hardware store on a more civilized world. The keeper sat up on a higher level that allowed the man to keep watch directly down a couple of aisles that Laney supposed held the more expensive goods.

"Seeking something in particular?" he called as she entered the gloom.

Not dark, but the sudden transition from daylight outside left her momentarily blind. Most likely a feature, not an aberration.

"Old books," Laney said, pausing before moving as her eyes adjusted.

"Fourth aisle," he called.

She followed, walking by the man's counter so he got a good look at her.

"Should I leave the bags here?" she asked.

He nodded and she slipped them onto the counter.

Money was in a pocket, along with her papers and such. That wasn't a purse so much as preparation in case she found something too big to fit in a pocket. He was welcome to look at a comb, a shemagh, and a few other things while she shopped.

The McLarens kept pace but didn't get hassled. Upper class folks hardly ever did, though Laney still suspected that she had more money than the McLarens did, as she could tap retirements and other investments.

It would be pointedly rude to ask if they were refugees or fugitives, much as she wanted to.

The library section was thin. Heavy on the sorts of escapist fiction that sailors on long circuits might buy to while away the hours. Nothing she found interesting, and more than a few she was already acquainted with.

She did pick up an extra key to wind her Analytical Engine. Somewhere, her old spare had vanished, and the thing was a collection of useless gears if you couldn't wind the spring to let you read scrolls.

Laney had no interest in trying to carve a block of brass to make a new one. Not unless it was critical.

Past that, she bought a glass bottle of water from a refrigerator, and suggested that the McLarens do the same, as the day was warm and dry. They agreed without really understanding, but that quite described the pair.

Outside, she began to work her way back towards the ship, wondering what a town like Astoria might have in store for her.

SCENE SEVENTEEN

Laney noted the time absently. Mid-afternoon, having skipped lunch after a heavy breakfast. She wouldn't say that she had picked Astoria clean, as she had only walked one half of one side of the long strip from where it intersected the main gate of the starport. The crowds had ebbed and flowed around them without much bother.

It would be rude to think of the two parts of this strip as fallopian tubes, but that was the image that came to mind when she considered it. Big, open square at the main gate, surrounded on all sides by bars and noise where sailors entered as a uterus. Where that left the starport itself and the ships therein was unfortunately no longer left to her imagination.

She snorted mostly to herself and chose not to share her thoughts with the McLarens. They'd been pleasant enough companions for the last few hours.

Then Brianna stepped close. A brush more than anything, as she was at the center of their threesome.

"We're being followed," she said so quietly that Laney almost missed it.

Laney was so shocked that she stopped moving and turned to the woman. It was like a stranger had taken up residence there in the last ten seconds. Then Brianna nodded, blinked, and turned back into the newlywed housewife of a surgeon.

Just like that.

Laney wanted to turn and look back but held herself facing forward. Began to walk again as if nothing had changed, a slow, meandering amble. Almost a saunter, if she was being saucy about it.

But Brianna had apparently seen something.

And Laney hadn't.

Laney moved them towards a bodega that seemed to appeal to sailors in a hurry to buy something, either just off the ship or running to board before departure. Cheap clothing. Sewing kits. Tools. All of it marked at least a quarter more expensive than the other end of the street.

Desperation pricing.

The window was glass, so it had bars set ten centimeters apart. Laney drew the McLarens close, as though having a conversation about the mannequin visible inside. Baggy black pants that might even fit Laney's butt without suspenders and a simple blue T-shirt as you wore under a tunic.

In reality, Laney was studying patterns of movement behind her. Sudden eddies in the current of bodies. In a river, those were rocks causing ripples and rapids. Here, two men had stopped walking long enough to cause traffic congestion and were again moving to get past Laney's party.

Intercepting them short of the big open market square that might be likened to a uterus in more ways than one.

Laney ignored those two after memorizing their faces. She wanted their friends. Two men wouldn't start trouble during the day, even in a place as rough as Astoria, without backup.

Perhaps they might think to mug the McLarens, but not Laney, even if she looked like a fat, old woman in a bright vest.

There. And there. Four of them, then. Not the four mercenaries that had been a problem at Weinsefeld Docks before departure. But then, Laney had been utterly amazed at how quickly *Last Stand* had made the journey here. Standard commercial shipping would still be at least another day out from arriving.

Captain Sladek had a fast ship and exceptional crew. Pity she wasn't here. And that Laney was without a firearm.

She would have to rely on her wits.

Not the first time doing that, either.

She turned to the McLarens.

"There are four of them I can note," she said quietly, as though asking if they wanted to go in and shop. "Two ahead. Two behind."

"Does Astoria maintain an adequate gendarmerie?" Constanz asked, highlighting how far from home that young man had wandered.

"I have not seen a deputy," Laney offered. And she had been looking. Measure of a town, especially a place like Astoria. Not poor, but certainly far from genteel.

"What would you suggest, then?" he asked.

"Follow me," she said. "Be prepared to run to the ship when I say so, because that might be necessary, and noise will hopefully cause our friends to withdraw from confrontation."

"Are we being mugged?" he gasped.

"They probably would like to think so," Laney growled.

That had been the *modus operandi* of the mercenaries at Weinsefeld, little good that it had done them.

Laney guided the McLarens back onto the street, making sure that she was between them and the near side where the two ahead had gone. She had little cash on her, and a man would have to be utterly desperate to look on her old bones with anything approaching lust, but Brianna McLaren upset all equations.

You might never encounter another human as stunningly beautiful if you lived to be two hundred.

Still, they had asked for her assistance today, and she had given it. Laney would see them safely back to the ship, though next time it might be better if Nakada traveled with them.

Only a fool would attempt his luck with that one.

Even with several friends.

The afternoon crowds had thinned in a way that had Laney considering a planetary culture of siestas. Nap through the heat of the day, then rouse later and go back to work. Certainly, the heat had come up some.

It gave her fewer places to disappear into the crowd, though it made the two men ahead of her more obvious.

They were not dressed as sailors, so they already stood out some. Ranch hands, perhaps, in heavy pants and boots with points designed to go into a saddle's stirrup. Shirt and vest like hers, but plain and worn, brown leather in the case of the vest and dirty gray shirt. Hats with wide brims, something that sailors didn't wear, because you hit them on things indoors.

Locals, then. Predators, still, but ambushers lurking by the water hole while they waited for their victims to come to them.

Laney considered tactics, and deliberately walked towards the two as they stepped off a boardwalk to approach. Armed, both of them. Revolvers as the Captain preferred, rather than the military ordnance that Nakada carried.

They were a little off guard at her approach, but not sufficiently. Laney still felt like pushing the confrontation now, when the McLarens might be able to run while she engaged her new friends. Old fat woman, perhaps, but still dangerous.

She felt the other two come out from behind her and close into a box.

"Going somewhere?" the taller man in front of her asked in a snarling, superior tone.

"*Nǐ xiǎng yào shénme?*" she snapped at the man in a vicious voice.

Chen. She'd spent time there a while ago and they had several languages generally unspoken in Arles or much of the Ergrove colonies. At least today.

Worked to throw the man off. Hard to be tough when someone might not speak the same language as you.

Out of the corner of her eye, Laney saw one of the men behind them put a hand on Brianna's shoulder. Possessive-like.

Before anybody could react, Brianna coiled up and horse-kicked him in the balls. She wasn't wearing heels of any height, but still had a leather walking sole.

That one went down painfully and Brianna stepped through the kick and backhanded the other one with a fist that sounded like a long wooden club to the jaw.

Laney wanted to be utterly shocked, but then training took over. The man in front of her had dropped a hand onto his pistol, mostly as a threat. She stepped up and drove a thigh into his groin, lashing out with her off-hand to grab the last one standing and pull him towards her before he awoke to trouble.

Number Four ended up in a headlock from which she could break his neck without a lot of effort if he gave her a reason.

"Why were you following us?" she growled in his ear, jerking things just enough to center his attention on living more than the next ten seconds.

Around them, the crowd had parted, but largely ignored the three men down. Only one was unconscious, but she had time before the other two could think again.

Brianna McLaren disarmed them both while everybody watched, holding two of the pistols with hammers drawn and barrels expertly centered. Her husband had the other two.

Laney didn't like the look in the woman's eyes. Hollow and black, like a shark rolling up to take a bite of you.

Nobody home but death.

"Just following orders," the prisoner gasped.

"Whose?" she asked.

"Masterson," he gasped when she squeezed.

Laney supposed that the Masterson Agency might be after Tessa Sladek and her crew. Little clues dropped that painted them in a more criminal setting than had been immediately obvious before leaving *Alfann*.

"I don't like you," Laney said, flexing her muscles with every syllable to ram that home. "If I ever see you again, they will never find your body. Look at my friend here. Does she look like she'd care if she cut you open and let you bleed to death right here in the street?"

Which was bad, because Brianna McLaren had exactly that look about her right now. Coldly lethal predatory beast. Take a bite out of your leg for fun, then come back after you stopped thrashing about.

"No, ma'am," her prisoner said.

"Do not ever come to Astoria again," Laney said plainly. "Next time I see you, you die. Do not ever mention me again, you or your friends. Do not talk about this incident, or I might have to come hunting you in the dark of night. *Do you understand me?*"

"YES!"

She stood, dropping him. Towered over the man's supine body, noting that Constanz McLaren had no idea how to hold a pistol, while his wife seemed to have been born with them in each hand.

Then Brianna lowered the hammers on her pair and handed one to Laney. Some spark passed in her eyes, and it was almost like the woman awoke from a deep sleep as a shiver passed from crown to heel.

"We should run," Brianna said in the voice Laney remembered.

Then Laney was chasing after her and Constanz, because they had neither of them even waited for her to nod.

She kept up, though Laney had the impression that Brianna held her pace for her husband.

Nobody followed. Laney made sure of that.

Someone was watching from the ship, though, because Captain Sladek was standing outside the cargo deck with her lever-action rifle in one hand as they got close, concern etched on her face.

Wyatt Nakada was nowhere to be seen. Laney wasn't fooled.

"Brianna, we're safe for now," Laney called.

She had to repeat it before the woman slowed. They were still jogging as they got there, but the Captain hadn't shouldered her weapon. That was good.

"Trouble?" Sladek asked, eyes on the horizon behind them.

"Issues in town as we were returning, Captain," Laney replied. "Best if we got indoors first, as I have questions for the McLarens as part of my explanation."

She turned to Brianna, but the woman's paleness wasn't the hard blush she expected. Same with Constanz.

"Wyatt!" Captain Sladek called. "In and lock it up!"

She turned and led them inside, where the air was cooler and the sunlight fallen to comfortable lighting.

Laney Coburn had many, many questions.

SCENE EIGHTEEN

Tessa had them all in the cargo bay, rather than headed forward to where it might be comfortable. Wyatt refused to be out of sight of the back door until he knew what was going on, and she tended to agree.

Something had changed with her passengers.

Fin and Maru had come aft to join them, so folks sat on trunks or leaned on ribs. Crew folks. The three new passengers were on stage, as it were. Even Abigail had moved to sit next to Fin and Maru.

"We had gone into town to do a bit of shopping," Laney began, before walking her story quickly and expertly through the usual crap and happenstance you got at a place like Astoria. "Then Brianna notified me that we were being followed."

The old woman pointedly paused there and turned to Brianna McLaren for an explanation that went beyond seeing someone suspicious. Such a term described at least half of Astoria.

McLaren had gone white. Or remained white. Jittery, but it wasn't exactly fear. And it wasn't the crash from being mugged, though none of them looked injured and they had four more pistols than they'd left with this morning.

Brianna opened her mouth. Nothing came out. Not even breath.

The air hung empty and heavy, like a cold morning in winter when you first woke up.

Constanz stepped up. Then realized he had a revolver in one hand like he was holding a live snake. Fool almost dropped it in the process of handing it to Fin.

"Sorry," he began. "I am not used to such things. Or to firearms."

He stopped there and sighed.

"You have to tell them," Brianna said, in a tone somewhere between authoritative and pleading.

Instead of answering, the man turned to his wife and some silent conversation took place. Tessa didn't hear anything, but she saw herself and Fin in the non-verbal back and forth.

So much you could say with body language alone.

Constanz McLaren admitted defeat. Or something.

"Are you certain?" he asked his wife, as though they were alone in the cargo bay.

"No, but I believe they will help," Brianna replied, glancing around as though seeing ghosts about her instead of people.

"Too much hinges on this," Constanz replied.

"And we may be out of options," Brianna replied.

Constanz shrugged. Then turned to face Tessa and Laney. His eyes were down and off to one side as he sought the words. Wouldn't be lies. No, this was too important, but he didn't know how to tell it.

Might never have told anyone these truths. And they would be truths, or their asses were back on the sand shortly and they could deal with local snakes or competing ships for passage.

"My name is not Constanz McLaren," he said simply.

As though *anybody* would be surprised by that revelation.

"When I bought these identities for the two of us, that was the best I could do," he said.

Then he shrugged and unbuttoned his blazer. From there, he started with the top button of his shirt under the ascot and undid four more to show what was underneath.

Binder. The sort of thing a woman with a small chest might wear to flatten her breasts entirely, so she gave off a silhouette that was at worst androgynous, and perhaps masculine.

"I am also not male," Constanz said. "That disguise was necessary to play a role, where those hunting us would not necessarily follow."

"And Brianna?" Tessa asked.

"My sister," Constanz grimaced. "We had thought it would be a simple disguise to maintain. After all, it had worked this long, getting us away from *Baramunz* and out of the entire Arles Region."

Tessa watched the woman button up her shirt again. Wyatt had stirred uncomfortably at the revelation, but he might have not been able to understand at the time why he found Constanz McLaren attractive, and been a bit confused.

Not like the big man had the emotional tools to deal with something that ambiguous. At least he wasn't likely to be any sort of sexual threat to either of the women. Man didn't necessarily have standards, after some of the barmaids she'd seen him with, but he was iron-clad about his ethics.

"You're Presley Horowitz," Fin said simply. "That's Nataliya."

Tessa watched both women jump. Wyatt and Maru did as well.

Tessa thought back to the picture. The wanted posters. Hand-drawn and simple. The sort of thing you could mimeograph off in places where electronic printers might be too expensive to own. Which described most of the Periphery, outside of some of the nicer Governors' palaces.

Whoever had done that sketch had used an old picture of Constanz but gotten most of the bones close. However, they'd given her long hair, thick and wavy in a manner similar to Brianna's.

Brianna McLaren, however…

The poster had shown the physical similarity between the two women. Bones and lines to the point that they might have been able to use the same ID photo when they were younger.

Laney had turned to Fin with her mouth about as fallen open as it would go. Catching flies, as Tessa's grandmother might have called it. She closed it now and moved to a trunk to sit.

Staggered, more than walked. Got settled and blinked too many times. Took the two pistols in her hands and set them somewhat out of reach, like she didn't want anyone thinking she was about to jump up and hijack the ship, arresting the fugitives for the reward money.

It was an awful lot of money.

Brianna, or perhaps Nataliya, moved up to stand next to Constanz/Presley. The bones in the torso were the same. And the legs. Brianna had a body like a dancer, and Constanz was a skinny guy. Girl. Something.

And neither of them had denied Fin's accusation. Tessa felt eyes turn her way as everyone waited for her to say something. *Captain* Sladek. Even her husband liked to remind folks that he was a happily kept man.

Because she was in charge.

"So you've had extensive plastic surgery," Tessa finally said to Brianna.

The woman's paleness had actually started to recede. Color was coming back into her face. She still only nodded, as if struck mute by something.

Must be big.

"What happened out there?" Tessa asked.

Again, Brianna's mouth opened. Closed. Pumped like a bellows but nothing came out. Constanz wasn't much help.

Tessa turned to Laney.

"I moved to confront the supposed muggers," Laney said. "As with the fools at Weinsefeld Docks, I thought that they might discount an old, fat woman and I could verbally disarm them. Or at least set them up for trouble. Then one of them touched Brianna without permission…"

Every head turned back to the beautiful woman. Tessa watched something happen in her eyes. A change. A subtle transformation.

Her stance suddenly changed as well, moving from the body language of indecision to that of a killer. Tessa had known enough of those in her day. There were at least two in the room with her.

The chin came out. The head up. The eyes gleamed with deadly intent.

"I was programmed with certain…*abilities*, Captain," Brianna finally said. Except that it wasn't Brianna speaking. Nataliya maybe.

Or Death herself.

"Go on," Tessa prompted.

Brianna might still be armed, but so was Tessa. And Wyatt.

"He touched me. That self-protection programming kicked in," Brianna said. "So I hurt him. And his friend."

"HA!" Laney interjected. "She back-kicked the one and knocked the other out on his feet with a single backhanded punch."

Tessa turned to Brianna, saw the woman nod. Almost a bow of the head in acknowledgment.

"She is correct, Captain."

"You said programmed," Fin spoke up, voice all friendly and curious, like he was going to Good Cop this.

Letting his wife play Bad Cop.

"That is correct, Mr. Barton," Brianna said.

"I'm Fin," he corrected her. "Remember that. You're among friends here. My father, may he live forever and a day, is *Mr. Barton*."

"Fin," Brianna nodded. Maybe even smiled a bit.

"Tell me about your programming," he said in a tone that induced storytelling, rather than being a demand.

"I can't," she said, suddenly shaky again. Shivering even.

Constanz stepped up and held her sister. Almost looked like the woman was about to collapse.

Then Abigail stood and moved to the other side, two women upholding the third. Maybe sharing warmth.

"She was…I suppose *kidnapped* is as good a term as anything," Constanz began in a quiet voice instead. "I graduated at the top of my class in med school. Top everything in every academic subject as a student before that. At least until she came along. My younger sister made me look like an idiot by comparison. Plus, she was already beautiful then. Dancer. Musician. Singer. Had the world ended up different, I could have seen her living a life like Abigail here does."

"She would have been amazing at it," Abigail nodded. "Who took her?"

"It was one of those schools for exceptionally gifted students on *Baramunz*," Constanz continued. "Best reviews. Full scholarship. Everything you might have learned, Abigail, with two other full *curriculae* on top of that. But something went wrong."

Brianna shivered so hard at those words that she nearly took both Abigail and Constanz over with her, but they managed to stay upright.

Tessa flashed back hard to the days in the camps, after *Vinoris*. Things that went wrong when men outnumbered women by such terrible ratios. And had size and anger on their side.

Tessa kept herself from growling, but only barely. Even Fin only knew slivers of those truths.

"As near as I can tell, they were a front," Constanz finally spoke after his sister settled a bit. "A group of former noblemen from Zaddinul, upset at losing the war to Lorastir and losing practically everything when the Emperor set a new aristocracy in place. Everything I have found in my research and bribes pointed to them building...*assassins*. Physically. Emotionally. Mentally. I used to get letters from her routinely, but they started getting weird. Talking about things that had never happened. Vacations we'd never been on. Planets we'd never visited. Old friends that existed only on those pages."

"A cry for help," Abigail said in the quiet that had fallen.

Constanz nodded to her.

"She can't talk much about it because they did things to her mind to prevent that," Constanz said. "Someone intended to turn my baby sister into the perfect killing machine, against her will. They broke her mind, then put it together again in a different order."

"Oh, no," Brianna suddenly spoke up, fire where she'd been ice before. "It's worse than that. They took out parts and replaced them with other things. There are mornings where I don't even recognize the face in the mirror, or the voices in my head. It is almost as though there are two or maybe five of me inside this skull."

"Why?" Fin asked delicately. Compassionately. It was Fin. He had that gift.

"She always looked like Lorastir aristocracy," Constanz said. "The particular shades of skin and hair that they venerate. All of those traits got accentuated, until any man—and most women—would be psychologically seduced before she spoke a word. Then they could get her in somewhere, kill her target, and escape afterwards. That much I was able to learn from folks I paid a stupendous amount of money to. The ones who found her. Who helped me break her out of that place before she was fully programmed and ready to be sent out. Still a virgin, at least in that way."

"So you have a clique of Zaddinul renegades still fighting the War?" Tessa asked.

"So it seems," Constanz shrugged. "I was a top surgeon on *Baramunz* busy being rich and famous and elite, so I didn't walk in the right circles. And a woman, when all of those I was able to identify were male. Almost all of their students were female, except for a few exceptionally pretty boys that were likely being programmed for a special kind of client."

Again, Tessa held the growl inside. Zaddinul had never been as progressive as anywhere else, when it came to the rights a woman might have over her own body. Of course, men like that would prey on pretty children and turn them into weapons, when they'd already lost the war.

Hell, *Baramunz* had fallen twelve years ago, and the final embers of active rebellion and revolution hadn't been crushed out until five years later at *Vinoris*.

At the *Last Stand*.

If then.

"Is she a threat?" Tessa asked in a hard voice, placing that question on a variety of levels.

"No," Constanz said in a matching adamantine tone. "Well, if someone tries to physically assault her, that programming surfaces, but like those assholes back there on the street, they'd have it coming at that point."

Tessa nodded. She'd known a lot of folks that had had it coming. A few she'd even delivered herself.

"So now what?" Tessa asked.

"I've been experimenting with some chemicals," Constanz said. "Injections that might help break her out of the things she's had done. I've seen some successes, but obviously we've been on the run for two years now, and things like that are harder to locate and acquire out here on the Periphery. I'd like to heal her. Failing that, I ask you for enough of a head start that we can maybe escape this planet and try our luck somewhere else."

"No," Tessa said flatly, snarling at all the cries of outrage around her, including Fin who she expected, but also Wyatt, who was not a soft-hearted man by any stretch of the imagination.

Tessa waved the hand not holding her rifle to get them to all shut up. Still took a bit.

"You are **not** leaving *Last Stand*, Constanz and Brianna McLaren," she continued. "I can't offer you much, but you're paying passengers willing to travel with us, wherever our jobs take us. Your words, by the way, not mine. I intend to hold you to that for a while."

She was grinning. Fin caught it first, but the smile spread out infectiously.

"Even though it puts you at risk?" Constanz asked.

"I was the one putting you at risk," Tessa countered with a harsh laugh. "We're smugglers, criminals, and any number of other accusations one might level at us. You folks were innocents from the Core who might have been a bit too delicate for this sort of thing."

That elicited more laughter. Relaxation. Brianna was standing now, rather than being held up by her smaller, older sister or the petite Abigail.

"What about me?" Laney asked now, a voice almost tiny with worry from such a big woman.

Tessa had almost forgotten about the older woman. Former soldier. Possibly a former spy for Lorastir.

Hopefully former.

Those two stolen revolvers were not in the woman's reach. Tessa and Wyatt didn't have guns pointed at her, but they could be there as soon as the woman moved. Even if she thought she was fast.

"What about you, Laney Coburn?" Tessa asked. "I seem to remember you saying that the War was over. Should be done and put in the past. That you were done being evil. Have you changed your mind?"

"Someone out there is building assassins, Captain," Laney said in a hard, ugly voice, eyes locked with Tessa to the point of ignoring the rest of the room. Like the McLarens and their ghosts earlier.

"That's Lorastir's problem," Tessa snapped back at her, just as sharp. "Seems to me if the Emperor didn't want enemies, he shouldn't treat some people so poorly."

"What do you mean?" Laney asked, surprised.

"The serfs only got new masters when Zaddinul fell," Tessa said. "Not freedom. Nothing else changed. If you're poor then you're a nobody. I got sucked up into their army at the end when a bunch of folks with guns decided that they needed more bodies to fight off Lorastir. Then they put me in camps after the *Last Stand*. Took me two years before I made it back to *Nulbuzir*. And found everything destroyed there. Or in the process of being torn down by the new masters when the old ones had been chased off or changed masters themselves. Managed to escape that shit and eventually made it to Hawkswold. Worked out here for a while, then went home and rescued Auntie Marusya. She's lost her entire family, until I'm all she has left, same as she's all I had before Fin. Lorastir and Zaddinul can deal with their own problems. There's no King Fyodor coming back from *Barakzir* with a magical sword in one hand to save everyone, okay?"

Tessa slammed her mouth shut. Most words she'd said on the subject in a long time. Maybe a bit of a fire in her belly on the topic of folks driven from home by greedy sons of bitches on *Baramunz* or *Falorea*. Or any so-called Capital System.

Lots of mouths fallen open around her. Even Fin, who really should have known better.

Auntie Maru nodded sagely. She had her own scars Tessa had never asked about. Losing a husband and four children to war, poverty, genocide, and starvation.

There were many reasons Tessa had that implant in her arm that kept her from getting pregnant for at least three more years. And why she'd get it replaced promptly.

"And we should just let the Arles Region go to hell?" Laney asked plaintively, all the fire bled out of her voice. And her eyes.

"It's Lorastir," Tessa countered angrily. "Do I look like

I care about their solid-gold toilets? Them folks have never been hungry. If they've forgotten the terrors of the Revolution, I can't help that they turned into the people they overthrew in the first place. Ergrove isn't much better. A genteel kind of intellectual poverty among their upper classes, but at least they don't bother me much, living in Hawkswold."

"So what should I do?" Laney asked.

"Nothing," Tessa replied. "Is that too much?"

The shock in the old woman's eyes was rather priceless, then it was gone a heartbeat later.

She mouthed the word *Nothing?* but no sound came out.

Tessa nodded.

Then Tessa let her own eyes turn hard.

"Or you can decide that you want to leave the ship," she continued. "Maybe try to collect the reward. That would be a bad idea."

"It would, Captain," Laney nodded sagely. "I'm good. Exceptional, even. Deadly and dangerous, living in a galaxy that strives to match me for that. I'm not as good as Brianna. Nobody is as good as Brianna, I suspect. I'm not dumb enough to try. And I'd like to stay with you. One of the questions I have been contemplating recently wasn't whether or not the many things I'd done in my time were good or evil. Now, I've seen a side of things hidden from me before. I was in service to evil. How deeply, though, have I been in service to that beast? And can I be redeemed from it?"

Constanz stepped away from Brianna now out of the corner of Tessa's eye. Turned to Laney Coburn.

"Do you wish to be redeemed?" Constanz asked quietly.

"Redeemed?" Laney asked. "Yes, but I don't know

how. Or where I fit in this galaxy. What I'm supposed to do. Where I might go."

"You'll go with us, Laney," Constanz said simply. "With all of us. Family is whatever you have to do to create it."

That was a far greater wisdom than Tessa would have attributed to the man. Woman.

Man. He needed to remain being Constanz McLaren, even in her mind, lest Tessa slip up at some point in conversation and leave a clue that might send hunters this way.

Laney studied the doctor, but made no untoward motions.

"Do you truly wish to be redeemed, Laney?" Abigail asked.

Like Constanz, she no longer needed to hold Brianna up, but stayed with the woman anyway. Warmth, if nothing else.

"I do," Laney said.

"Then perhaps you should consider all of this your penance," Abigail said.

Tessa kept her mouth shut. Abigail already saw *Last Stand* and its crew as a project of redemption.

She was not wrong in that assessment.

"Penance?" Laney managed.

Whatever pithy observation Abigail was about to offer disappeared as someone banged on the damned passenger door of the cargo hold.

Every person, it seemed, was suddenly holding a gun on that door.

SCENE NINETEEN

Tessa took a deep breath and thumbed the hammer on her rifle back down.

Everybody was maybe a bit too twitchy.

And Fin was down here, instead of up on the bridge watching the landing cameras, or he might have seen someone coming, like he had when it had been the others running for their lives.

"Abigail, get in your shuttle right now," Tessa ordered. "McLarens, you go with her in case you need to get away from Astoria while this gets sorted out."

Laney had gotten to one of those revolvers and covered the door amazingly fast. She turned to look a question at Tessa.

"I could use an extra gun, if this turns into a firefight on my deck," Tessa told the woman. "Fin, you and Maru get upstairs and prep for flight, in case we have to isolate some asshole here and leave all his friends on the ground behind."

He nodded and started jogging, revolver still in hand, where it might be one hell of a surprise later.

With any luck, it would never come to that, because whoever it was would get to Fin over her dead body.

And a few others.

Tessa, Wyatt, and Laney. Armed to the teeth. Twitchy as hell.

She turned to Wyatt first.

"Vanish," she ordered.

He nodded, set *Doomripper*'s safety, and got to work. Man occasionally rearranged the cargo bay to keep his lines of fire and hiding holes just so. It was like he went to bed every night thinking about all the ways someone might try to storm the ship. And how he'd kill every single dog of them in the response.

Tessa considered her rifle, then moved to the arms locker and put it away. She was faster with the revolver anyway.

She turned to Laney, caught the shift in readiness about the woman. Old soldier was suddenly at the forefront, ready to march or kill.

Tessa nodded and moved to the rear hatch. She keyed the intercom, then locked it open so every word spoken here would be relayed to Fin and Abigail.

Just in case.

Deep breath. Flex the hands once to loosen them. Pop the neck.

Shift to the side of the hatch, where someone rushing it couldn't tackle her. Laney was about five meters away in a dueling stance that had the pistol aimed where the fool would be when he stopped in confusion and stood up.

Tessa keyed the hatch open, revolver in hand and ready to pistol whip the first dumb sonbitch that came through.

Nothing.

"Hello?" a voice asked from outside.

Tessa followed her barrel around the edge and pointed it and eyes at the outside.

Young man standing there. Hands came up defensively.

"Oh, hey, not like that," he said.

Took her a moment, then Tessa finally recognized him. Not one of the goons from Bao Li's shop, but he had been standing off to one side watching and listening. Younger fellow. Not as big as the bouncers. Better dressed. Had an air of an executive assistant about him, rather than *goon*.

"Help you with something?" Tessa asked.

He had a small cart behind him. Really more of a children's wagon than anything, but wider and longer. And two more goons from Bao Li's place with him. Two of the bouncers who had been so intent on hemming her in. Faces she knew.

"Bao Li sent me," he offered carefully. "Nobody was answering the ship's comm, so she sent me direct. It's about that cargo of yours?"

After the rest of her day, it took Tessa a few moments to figure out what the hell the man was talking about.

She studied the two bouncers.

"You two wait out here," she said simply, pistol only accidentally pointed at the bigger one.

They nodded, uncertain as to what was going on.

Hell, Tessa was uncertain.

"You," she said to the other man. "In. And bring your cart."

She stepped back. By the time she turned around, Laney was standing off to one side like a passenger that had wandered aft at the wrong moment, instead of a killer prepared to empty her stolen pistol into someone coming aboard.

Wyatt was still invisible, but that was his thing.

Fellow stepped across her threshold with his wagon in tow, looking a mite skittish. Tessa didn't do anything to assuage his feelings. Then she closed the hatch behind him and locked it again.

Just in case.

The man came to rest in the middle of the open space.

"Uhm, you do still have the cargo for sale?" he asked in a carefully neutral voice.

"Do," Tessa replied. "Hadn't made arrangements with anybody for a price or delivery instructions, so I'm a bit put out that you and your friends showed up at my door unannounced. Uninvited."

He bowed formally to her now, folding at the waist.

"My apologies, Captain Sladek," he said on rising. "As noted, nobody was answering, so my boss suggested that I should endeavor to determine if there was a problem. I brought some friends, just in case. It appears, however, that things are well?"

"Had a bit of a problem with some locals earlier," Tessa said. "Tried to mug my passengers. Was just trying to decide if I should go give them a ration of grief over it. Hey, what's your name, anyway?"

"Qulu Azad," he said with a wry, twisted grin.

Tessa caught the play on words. Out in some of the older languages you found on rim worlds, it translated roughly as "Free Servant" without telling you his real name.

Lots of folks on the Periphery didn't use real names. Tessa didn't have any enemies left from the old days that she was aware of.

Or friends.

Azad turned to Laney and sized her up.

"Problems with locals?" he asked. "In broad daylight?"

So Laney described the four fellows again. Sounded

like ranch hands into the big city for some fun. Maybe got hired on the spot by some Masterson Op to do things. Or just be assholes.

Lots of folks would cut you a deal for that sort of thing.

Tessa watched Azad. Seemed a bright fellow.

"I shall make inquiries," he said sternly, suggesting that maybe Laney's threat wasn't all those fellows had to worry about. "However, I came about the cargo. Are you still dealing, Captain?"

"Didn't set a price with Bao Li," Tessa growled at the man.

"Oh!" he replied. "My apologies. She located the original buyer and took over the contract from Raven. I would like to reach into my pocket for a bag of coins for you. Preferably without being shot in the process."

Tessa realized that she was still dead-centered on the man's chest with her revolver. She dropped the hammer quietly and slipped it onto her thigh.

"Sorry," she said. "Go ahead."

He was in baggy pants and a loose tunic. Muted green. Layers against heat and probably waterproof, depending. One hand went into a front pocket and came out with a felt bag that looked heavy.

"I am aware that your original contract was for three ducats," Azad said as he handed it to her. "However, Bao Li took a lesser percentage for herself as appreciation for you and your honesty, Captain, so there are thirty-five yuan here and a hope that you might be amenable to future contracts."

Thirty-five wouldn't make her rich, but it would help with maintenance. And other things. Especially with more paying passengers aboard. Doubly so if folks were certain that the Horowitz renegades were in Hawkswold Sector.

It went into a pocket for now.

"Stuff's hidden," Tessa said simply. "If you'll give us a few moments while you wait with your friends on the front porch, we'll dig it out and roll the wagon to you."

"Excellent," Azad said, bowing again.

He immediately turned back to the hatch and waited for her to unlock and open it, stepping through before it was even fully open.

Tessa closed it again and shrugged.

"That was weird," Wyatt said as he appeared from behind a stack of old boxes.

"Yup," Tessa agreed. "However, I'm fine dealing with Bao Li if Raven's permanently out of the picture. And she seems to have a pretty good impression of me. That or the cargo was worth way more than Raven led me to believe."

"Should you have asked for more in that case, Captain?" Laney asked.

"I got hired to do a thing." Tessa turned to the woman and speared her eyes. "A contract for goods acquired and delivered, at an agreeable price. Raven's deal, but I told Bao Li about it, and she honored it. More than honored it. But it was a contract, and I will keep those."

The older woman nodded in understanding.

"Now, you get sworn to secrecy, Laney," Tessa grinned at the woman's sudden confusion.

"Why is that?" Laney replied. "I mean, yes, I intend to keep all these secrets. But why?"

Tessa nodded to Wyatt and they moved to the sidewall where a couple of hidden latches opened an old maintenance crawlspace, pulling aside the front so they could both reach in and grab the crate with the iridium.

About forty kilograms of deadweight mass, and awkward, so it took both of them to lift it onto the wagon and get the thing arranged just so.

Wyatt moved back to cover but didn't vanish. Aimed his rifle at the hatch and smiled.

Tessa rolled her eyes, but Wyatt was Wyatt. Once you understood that, the rest was much easier.

"Stepping out to deliver the cargo," she said, popping open the hatch.

Azad and his two bouncers were there. Tessa handed him the controls to the wagon and slipped off to one side.

"Thank you, Captain," he said. "In the interests of everyone involved, I shan't open it here where prying eyes might covet it, so I shall take you at your word. Will you be in Astoria for long?"

"Need to buy some things with my windfall," Tessa said. "Maintenance and the like. Maybe a pretty dress, just because. I expect we'll be around for most of a week, depending. Should I call on your boss before departure?"

"That would be most excellent, Captain," Azad nodded. "Until then."

The man turned to his goons and nodded. One led and one trailed, while Azad guided the wagon. Not exactly priceless, but twenty-four bars of Tool-grade iridium was a nice treasure in the right hands.

Not Tessa's. She didn't even have tools to work such a metal. You needed a reasonable-sized foundry for that. And a lot of need.

Instead, she stepped back and closed the hatch.

"We're clear," she announced. "Visitors are departing."

"They really likely to go hunting those fool cowboys?" Fin asked from the bridge.

"I hope so," Tessa said.

"Why is that, Captain?" Laney asked.

"Astoria could be a nice place," Tessa replied. "I'm not all that keen about the authorities arresting all the brokers and fixers, because the economy would collapse overnight, but not having to walk around with a gun on my hip all the time would be a pleasant change."

Laney nodded.

"*Baramunz* can be like that," she said. "And *Falorea*."

"Both, I'm certain, are lovely places," Tessa said. "For someone with pale skin and much lighter hair. Not for me. I'd rather make a living out here."

"Are you ever likely to return to the Arles Region?" Laney asked.

"There's nothing for me there," Tessa said. "Only lost dreams best left buried."

"Lost dreams, Captain?" Laney pressed.

"Lost everything," Tessa acknowledged. "Gone and buried. As Constanz said, family is whatever you have to do to make it. All the family I have left is aboard this ship."

Laney wanted to scoff at that. It was there in her eyes. Still, the woman held her tongue.

Like the McLarens, she might have also finally found a place she belonged.

Read More

Be sure to read the rest of the Last Stand series!

https://www.knottedroadpress.com/product-category/last-stand

About the Author

Blaze Ward writes science fiction in the Alexandria Station universe (Jessica Keller, The Science Officer, The Story Road, etc.) as well as several other science fiction universes, such as Star Dragon, the Dominion, and more. He also writes odd bits of high fantasy with swords and orcs. In addition, he is the Editor and Publisher of *Boundary Shock Quarterly Magazine*. You can find out more at his website www.blazeward.com, as well as Facebook, Goodreads, and other places.

Blaze's works are available as ebooks, paper, and audio, and can be found at a variety of online vendors. His newsletter comes out regularly, and you can also follow his blog on his website. He really enjoys interacting with fans, and looks forward to any and all questions—even ones about his books!

Never miss a release!

If you'd like to be notified of new releases, sign up for my newsletter.

http://www.blazeward.com/newsletter/

Buy More!

Did you know that you can buy directly from the KRP website?

https://www.knottedroadpress.com/shop/

About Knotted Road Press

Knotted Road Press publishes dynamic fiction set in exotic locations and unique non-fiction voices in genres such as autobiography, business, cookbooks, and how-to. Our authors cover a wide range of genres including science fiction, fantasy, mystery, literary, and poetry, appealing to all readers. We offer both DRM-free ebooks and print books for a global readership.

Knotted Road Press
www.KnottedRoadPress.com
www.KnottedRoadPress.com/Shop

www.ingramcontent.com/pod-product-compliance
Lightning Source LLC
Chambersburg PA
CBHW070551100726
47907CB00004B/1343